THE WARNINGS

Margaret Buffie

KIDS CAN PRESS LTD.

TORONTO

Kids Can Press Ltd. acknowledges with appreciation the assistance of the Canada Council and the Ontario Arts Council in the production of this book.

Canadian Cataloguing in Publication Data

Buffie, Margaret
        The warnings

Previously published under title: The guardian circle.
ISBN 1-55074-251-5

I. Title. II. Title: The guardian circle

PS8553.U453W37   1994   jC813'.54 C94-931951-1
PZ7.B84Wa 1994

This novel was previously published under the title *The Guardian Circle*.

Kids Can Press Ltd.
29 Birch Avenue
Toronto, Ontario, Canada
M4V 1E2

Edited by Charis Wahl
Printed and bound in Canada by Webcom

94 0 9 8 7 6 5 4 3 2 1

To the Buffie girls who once lived at 1241

THE WARNINGS

Chapter 1

When my dad dropped me off that October day in front of his Aunt Irene's, I'd already decided that the next few months were going to be a colossal pain. When I got my first look at the house, it became a certainty. When my two old suitcases hit the wet pavement beside the truck, I could feel a big door starting to close on me. When I saw the look on Dad's face, it slammed shut.

He was sitting high in the cab of his eighteen-wheeler. Under the crumpled peak of his baseball cap, his eyes looked sad. I didn't think it was an act. Not entirely, anyway. I knew he wasn't about to change his mind either. I also knew deep down inside that he was relieved. Now he wouldn't have to worry about me any more. He was free. I squinted up at him and felt my jaw tighten. I'd finished with arguing. I'd

1

finished with pleading. I'd pretty well finished with everything. Let him go ahead and do whatever he wanted. And if he was feeling lousy about it, then good.

"Are you sure you don't want me to walk you to the door?" he asked, peering down at me through the drizzling rain.

I shrugged. "Why bother? You better get going. Don't want to be late getting out on the Great Highway to Nowhere."

The truck grumbled deep in its belly, before releasing a huge wheezing sigh. It inched forward with a snort of black smoke. Dad frowned, pulled his cap forward and rubbed a hand over his mouth.

"Come on, Rach, that's not fair," he said. "You know I had to do it this way. I'll be back before you know it. We'll work something out. I promise."

That was the point we'd been arguing about, you see. I didn't think he had to do it this way at all. And how did I know if or when he'd be back? I'd heard the same promises from my mother Joanna. And I hadn't seen her in months.

"Hey, forget it," I said through clenched teeth. Why didn't he just take off? That's what he wanted to do. Didn't he? A gust of wind shook the trees above, splattering raindrops across the truck's roof. "Go ahead."

"Okay. Right. I will. And you'll be fine." He sounded as if he was trying to convince himself instead of me. "Go on now, honey. Or you'll get soaked. I'll call. As soon as I can. I *have* to go."

He lifted the arm that was hanging out of the window and waved. With another cough and grumble the truck moved steadily off, its tail-flaps catching the spray from the puddles along the road. At the end of the street, it signalled a left turn and edged around the corner.

"You *have* to go. Right. Have a great escape, Dad," I muttered. "Good job, Rachel. Two parents down. None to go. Not bad for an only kid. I should hire myself out. No parent too tough."

There was nothing to do now but face the tall house across the street. When Dad's old aunt had visited us at the farm, she'd described it as a stately home. Well, it might have been stately once, but now it was something else altogether — a crumbling pile of bricks the colour of raw beef liver. The whole dump stood in a yard of tangled yellowing weeds and wild hedges. Around it stood a circle of oak trees, their crooked branches twisting up into a dark grey sky. *Nightmare on Elm Street* before my very eyes.

Leafless vines, like liquorice whips, crawled all over the old bricks. Probably the only things holding it all together. A big open veranda staggered along the front of the house and around one side. Rain slid down a deep sway in its roof onto the steps. All around me was the wet smell of rotting leaves.

"This is great. *This* is just terrific." I pulled my hood forward to keep my glasses from spotting up any worse. "I wonder if Count Dracula knows about this joint."

Sometimes joking helps. Sometimes it doesn't.

I walked toward the house under a ceiling of street elms. Suddenly, it was hard to breathe. I wanted the open prairies and wide skies I knew. How could I face a winter in a city? Here, only patches of grey sky cut through the jumble of leaves. Where could I run or bike or just get away from things in a place crammed with buildings and stop signs and red lights?

Ahead of me the house and black oaks shifted behind the drizzle, looking darker and taller at the same time. Shadows — from the trees? — flickered across the top storeys of the house.

I shook my head and closed my eyes. Please not here, not now. Let me get through this stay without Weird Feelings and Warnings. I'd had enough of them to last a lifetime. And lately it had got worse. Sometimes I felt as if I was walking around with a tight bundle of nerves in each hand — afraid to hold them because they hurt so much and afraid to drop them in case I melted away. I opened my eyes and stared at the house. I had the prickly feeling that someone was staring at me from inside. I clenched my hands open and shut, feeling for the handles of the suitcases, needing something solid and real under my fingers.

"This is stupid," I ground out. "My imagination has gone berserk again. I won't let it happen. I will not let some stupid old house and some stupid old woman scare me." I kicked a pile of leaves near the curb and stubbed my toe. "Oow! Oow! *Oow!* I hate this. I absolutely hate this. I'll go in there and if I don't like it, I'll leave. That's what I'll do. Leave!"

Big words. I had only a few dollars Dad had given me. The rest had gone to Aunt Irene for my upkeep, he'd said. Where could I go on sixteen dollars and twelve cents? I stomped up the stairs and pushed the doorbell. Long and hard. One week. I'd give her one week. And then what? a little voice asked. I'll face that when I come to it, I answered. More big words.

Chapter 2

A distant jangle sounded behind the door. I shifted back and forth in my sneakers, squishing cold water between my toes and working myself up. Where was she? It was bloody freezing out here. I was about to poke the bell again when the door creaked open a few inches and a large bulging eye peered out. It looked me up and down, batted its eyelashes a few times and disappeared.

This was definitely not Aunt Irene. The door opened a fraction wider and this time a quivering purple mouth joined the eye. "I'll take two, honey," it said, "but feel them for the nuts."

"Two?" Nuts? What was going on? Who was she talking to? I looked over my shoulder. I was alone on the veranda.

"Yeah, two of the half-pounders," the mouth continued, "and make sure they're loaded with nuts. They get chintzier and chintzier with those things every year."

"Look . . . I'm not — "

"With those bags, you must have quite a pile to sell. So, I'll take three on second thought. I love my chocolate."

That's when it dawned on me. The eye and mouth thought I was selling chocolate bars for school. "Look, I'm not selling anything. I'm Rachel MacCaw. Irene MacCaw's niece. Doesn't she live here? Isn't this 135 Cambric Street?"

Maybe Dad had got his streets mixed up and Aunt Irene actually lived in a perfect little white house one street over. No such luck. The door swung open. The woman behind it was five feet tall and just about as wide. She wore a purple flowing thing — part housecoat, part tent — that hung down to her ankles. Below that she had on a pair of tiny purple slippers. How did she keep all that fat standing upright? She looked as if a poke from my little finger would up-end her.

"Rachel? Holy mackerel!" she crowed. A pile of pink curls on top of her head bounced and wobbled. "Now how could I have forgotten? Not doing my job, that's what. But wait! You weren't due until next weekend. Were you?"

I shrugged. "My dad's got a load to deliver to B.C. He called Aunt Irene last night. I'm only one week early."

"She didn't tell *us*, did she now? We'll have to do something about that silly Irenie, won't we? Likes to keep us in the dark. On our toes. Well, never mind, come in, come in."

7

The woman seemed to know who I was. But who the heck was she? Didn't Aunt Irene live here alone?

"I'm Mitzi, dear," she said, as if reading my mind. "Mitzi Dubbles, late of the Red River Revelations and Circus Performers Agents Co. Inc." She leaned forward and looked up and down the street before grabbing my arm and hauling me into the house. "We've been looking forward to this. My heavens, haven't we?"

She snapped a whole bunch of shiny new locks on the inside of the door before leading the way into a gloomy hallway. All those locks weren't going to help if I decided to make a run for it. I glanced around. One whole wall was covered with maroon wallpaper spotted with water stains. On it in a straight line hung a long row of dark shiny oil paintings. A tall staircase took up the other wall. Under its shadow was a black door with a rounded top. Probably a cupboard full of hairy-armed spiders. The whole place smelled like mouldy dishrags.

"Do you live here, too?" I demanded, hoping the answer would be no. One old woman was going to be rotten enough to live with, never mind two.

Mitzi Dubbles opened her mouth, but another voice answered for her. Thin and dry as dust, it drifted down from above. We looked up. A skull, outlined in a halo of fuzzy hair, hung over the second-storey banister. It grinned, showing two rows of long yellow teeth. The tight skin under the pointed cheekbones sank into the deep shadows. I took a step back. A long bony hand waved at us.

"Didn't that naughty Irenie mention Mitzi and me?" he asked. "Well, never mind, because now you've met the husband-and-wife team of — awk!"

He suddenly fell forward, thrashing the air and landing in a crumpled heap of skinny arms and legs on the bottom step.

"Hey! Call an ambulance!" I shouted, dropping my suitcases and running to him. "He's probably broken something!" If he isn't already dead, I added to myself.

When I didn't hear gasps or screams or even running footsteps, I looked over my shoulder. The fat woman was unwrapping a toffee. She stuffed it into her puffpastry face. I stared at her.

"Luther, stop it," she said in a gummy voice. "You're scaring her, you silly man."

I swung around and stared at him.

"Hee, hee," cackled Luther Dubbles, unwinding himself and sitting up. "I've still got it, Mitzi, my pet. I've still got it."

I looked from one to the other and then to the padlocked door, my mind racing. Were they crazy? Who were they? And where was Aunt Irene? Did she look after them, was that it? Was this a nursing home for nutty pensioners? For a fraction of a second I saw the funny side of it. If this was a nut house, I'd fit in perfectly. As nutty as these two looked, I bet they didn't hear voices or see things that weren't there the way

9

I did. A nut house. Perfect. Just perfect. I stood up and glared at Luther Dubbles, my hands on my hips. Loony-bin or not, I wasn't about to put up with any crap.

"What are you *doing*?" I demanded, my voice squeaking.

"Shocked the socks off you, didn't I, girl?" He grinned, his long yellow teeth taking up most of the bottom of his grey face. He sat forward and looked me over carefully. "Not at all what we expected. But feisty, eh, Mitzi? That's good. The red hair's a good sign, too. In fact, you might just be the ticket. Whaddya say, Mitz?"

I had absolutely no idea what he was yapping on about. Or why he kept grinning like that. He looked positively demented.

Mitzi popped another candy through the purple circle, smacked her lips and said, "Come on, honey, let's go hunt down your auntie now that Luther here's had his fun."

She shoved a handful of wrapped toffees at me but I shook my head. "No? Hey, don't let Luther worry you. He tries that on practically everyone. His acrobat years, see? Isn't he terrible? Luther, you're just terrible!" She flapped both pudgy hands in his direction, scattering toffees all around.

"I'll see you at dinner then," said Luther. "Meanwhile, I've got some important documents to go through." He gave us a last horrible look at his teeth before sprinting back up the stairs two at a time.

"Important documents, my eye," said Mitzi.

"He's got the latest Stephen King up there. Follow me, kiddo."

I left my suitcases where they were for a quick getaway and followed the purple tent down the hall. When we reached the door at the end, Mitzi stopped.

"Listen, kiddo," she said in a low voice, "before we go in there, I've gotta tell you that I think poor Gladys has botched up another dinner. So, for Pete's sakes don't say anything. She'll only bawl her head off and we'll get nothing to eat at all. Okay? See?"

It wasn't okay. "Who's Gladys? I thought Aunt Irene lived here alone."

"You did? Hah! That's a good one. We're all in this and have been since we found the place. It took us ages to find it. And who'd believe what some crooks ask for a house nowadays? An arm and a leg, that's what! We had to pool our money and then some."

This did not sound good. "So Aunt Irene lives here with you and Mr. Dubbles. And this Gladys. Is that all?" I demanded.

"Oh no! We have Mr. Basely, the dearie. And we're stuck with Gladys's grandkid for a bit. A bit too long, if you ask me! And what a useless twit she is. I hope you intend to help around here and not just eat your head off." She poked holes in the air around my head with one short finger.

Just who did this fat biddy think she was — ordering me around? I narrowed my eyes and said, "Look, I know what's right and what's wrong, you know. I may have been brought up on a farm, but I didn't live in the barn!" I could feel my ears burning. They do that when I'm mad.

Mitzi tapped me on the arm with the same podgy finger. "Right you are, eh? Follow me, kiddo." She turned and pushed open the kitchen door.

I guess I'd expected a come-back. Instead, she kept nodding and smiling and I ended up feeling kind of stupid. Which ticked me off even more. I slouched into the kitchen behind her. The stink of burned meat and boiled cabbage rolled forward to meet us. Just right for my mood. Perfect.

The kitchen was big, with a row of small-paned windows along the back wall. They looked out over a misty yard of dripping trees and spiky bushes. In one corner of the room, around the stove, hung a huge thick cloud of wavering smoke. Aunt Irene stood in the middle of it, poking at a smouldering chunk of charcoal in a grubby blue roaster. I put my hand over my nose and muttered, "Jeez!"

Another woman sat at a huge work table in the middle of the room, mopping her eyes with a red apron. "It's useless, isn't it?" she sobbed. "I seem to be quite unable to make anything in that stove without ruining it completely. Utterly, utterly useless. It's that oven, you see."

"The top of the stove doesn't seem to work for her, either," Mitzi murmured in my ear.

"And I was so sure this roast beef would be just right," continued the woman in the red apron. "Now the potatoes and carrots I put around it have simply disappeared and all is lost, all is lost," she moaned.

"Oh, never mind that, Gladys," said Mitzi. "Guess who's here?"

Aunt Irene looked up. "Rachel! When did you get here? It was getting so late, I thought Alan may have changed his mind. You or he should have phoned me to say you would be late."

"Now, Irenie, take it easy. She just got here, after all," said Mitzi, opening the back door and pushing it back and forth on its hinges. The smoke moved in tattered clumps towards freedom. I wanted to follow them. "Luther did his stair routine for her."

"Did he now, the silly idiot," said Aunt Irene, pursing her lips and pointing to the table. "Rachel, you sit over there until I get a grip on things here."

I dragged out a wooden chair and slumped down across from the strange little woman in the red apron. This one was the opposite of Mitzi Dubbles — small and skinny with short straight grey hair scraped back from her raisin-wrinkled face with two big red barrettes. Snuffling softly to herself, she lowered a pair of rhinestone-studded glasses from their perch on the top of her head. Her nose was like a big lump of Silly Putty. It almost touched her chin. She smiled wetly from behind the skinny oval lenses and wobbling nose as if about to tell me a secret.

"You wear glasses, too, I see," she said in a small ragged voice. "How nice . . . I mean, nice that we both wear glasses. I bought these over thirty years ago, at Woolworth's . . . or was it

13

Oretski's . . . why, I've worn any number of them since I was your age, and my, you've got red hair, don't you?" She stopped and took a gulp of air. "I like that, it's very good, didn't the other one have red hair, too, Irenie? You told me that, didn't you? What . . . what I mean is . . ." She glanced at Aunt Irene nervously. "Well . . . just that it's very nice hair, isn't it, I mean to say . . ." She looked at me. "I'm the cook here, did they tell you?"

I didn't say anything. I was still wondering about the red hair business. Hadn't Luther Dubbles said the same thing? Did they all talk gobbledygook or was there a reason for mentioning my hair colour? A colour I don't mind telling you I've hated since day one.

"Never mind that now, Gladys," snapped Aunt Irene. "As far as this dinner goes, I think I can make a fairly presentable stew out of it. I'll be right back. Rachel, come along, I'll show you to your room."

I stood up.

"No!" cried Gladys. I sat down. "Oh, I didn't mean you, Rachel dear. You can stand up again. No . . . what I mean, Irene dear, is that I promised to pay my way by being housekeeper and cook. I couldn't stay otherwise, I just couldn't."

"But you didn't tell us you couldn't cook, Gladys," said Mitzi, shutting the back door. "You didn't mention *that*."

"But I've always been a good cook, up until I went into that dreadful old age home . . . that horrible place. I miss my garden. I've just forgotten a few things, but I'll get better, I know I

14

will . . ." She looked around vaguely as if the answer might be floating somewhere in the air around her head. A real loony-tune.

"Yes, well, in that case, we'll both do something about it," said Aunt Irene. "We'll use those packaged gravies I bought you."

"And for Pete's sakes, follow the directions this time, Gladys," added Mitzi, "so we don't end up with brown paste again. And we don't want none of your Yorkshire pudding, either. And put out lots of bread and . . ."

The swinging door cut off Mitzi's orders. As mixed up and tired and cheesed-off as I was, I couldn't help feeling a little sorry for the one named Gladys. Why did the other two treat her like that? As if she was senile or something. Maybe she *was* senile. Great. Just great. A house full of either bossy or loony old coots. One as bad as the other.

When and if my father ever called, I'd have a thing or two to tell him. And I knew I wouldn't hold back on what I thought of a parent who would do this to his only daughter, either!

Chapter 3

Well, one thing was definite. Aunt Irene wasn't acting the same as she had when she visited the farm. She'd been sticky nice then, like syrup on your fingertips. Now, as I followed her down the dimly lit hall, she reminded me of one of those snooty types in a dress shop who know you don't have enough money and who leave you standing in the middle of the floor staring around like a dope.

Maybe she'd been putting on an act for Dad's sake in August. But why? It wasn't as if she'd *had* to take me. Hadn't Dad kept saying that this whole moving to Winnipeg idea had been hers, not his?

I stopped dead in my tracks. What if he'd lied? What if he had been the one to arrange it? Maybe he'd even begged her to take me — or worse yet, paid her. I glared at the backs of her square sensible shoes as they marched on ahead of me. Something squeezed tight in my chest. Suddenly I really hated her, with her long thin legs, her thick straight waist, her tightly rolled black and silver hair. Who needed some witch who looked as if someone had dipped her in starch? The shoes started up the same wide set of stairs that Luther Dubbles had fallen down. I picked up my suitcases and dragged behind, kicking the backs of the treads with my toes.

When we reached the second floor, I stared miserably down the long dingy hall. A grimy window, overlooking the street, dripped with rain. What a dump.

"This room on the left is mine," said Aunt Irene, leading the way down the hall. "Gladys's is at the far end, Mr. Basely's is over there, and the Dubbles are in the middle on the left. There's another room here on the right, but we're expecting a new . . . er . . . tenant sometime soon, so . . . of course . . ." She looked over her shoulder as if someone was creeping up on us.

I frowned. Great. Another fossil would be moving in. Maybe this one pulled pennies out of his nose. Still, I have to admit that I moved pretty quickly past the Dubbles' door when we passed by, expecting the skull head with its horrible grin to appear around the corner like a dried apple on a stick.

When Aunt Irene reached an archway cut in the wall, she stopped, straightened her belt and smoothed the silver wings over her ears. I stared at the peeling wallpaper and dragged my feet.

"Don't scuff the carpet, please," she said,

sharply. "The threads are thin enough. Now. These stairs are yours." She turned and began walking up a steep-pitched narrow flight. "Of course, we have a great deal to do on the house. Terribly neglected, as you can see."

The carpet on the stairs wasn't as worn as in the rest of the house, but the air became colder the higher we got.

"Now, I've put you up here on your own. You're old enough to manage. The people who owned 135 before us ran it as a boarding-house for over forty years, but they rarely used the attic because . . . well . . . it was quite cold in the winter and hot in the summer." She looked down at me and her stiff face changed — even her voice softened a little. "You *are* young, aren't you? Almost sixteen? When I was at the farm, I hadn't noticed how . . . well, how . . . small you were. Still we've given you a couple of good heaters up here, and I'm sure you'll do very well . . . yes, from what I've seen so far, you'll manage. I only hope . . . well, we'll see how you do, shall we?" She smiled with a faint twist of the lips before turning and continuing up the stairs. Yeah, I thought, we'll see if I can stand the bunch of *you*.

The stairway turned near the top and landed in a big open room. The ceiling had more angles than my geometry book. A brown metal bed stood under the narrow window not far from the stair railing. It was covered with a new yellow quilt — the only bit of colour in the cold grey room. In the middle of a faded oriental rug

18

stood two spring-sagged armchairs made of dusty coloured velvet.

The only other pieces of furniture, a desk and wooden chair, stood in front of an arched window inside a small nook. On the wall facing the street were two long pointed windows. Masses of vines ran up and down and across all the windows except the one beside the bed. All it had was a thin streaky film of dirt.

I pressed my forehead against its coldness. This window looked down onto the side yard. I could see bits of both the front street and back lane and slices of other tall houses nearby. Everything outside looked wet and grey and depressing, too.

"There's a big cupboard for your clothes over there," said Aunt Irene, pointing to a tiny door tucked inside a small alcove. "Take no notice of that door on the inside wall. It leads to the other part of the attic, a store-room. I don't want you messing about in it." She sat down on the bed and patted the yellow comforter. "Take off your slicker, Rachel, and sit down. I want to talk to you."

I dropped my raincoat over the stair railing, edged towards the bed and sat down at the far end. My eyes travelled around the damp cold cave, taking in its faded-rose wallpaper and shadowed corners. Then, like an inner slide show, pictures began flashing on and off in my mind — Dad's long solemn face looking over his shoulder as he waved goodbye; my old room on the farm with its shelves of toys and books; and

19

then strongest of all, Joanna's thin wide-eyed face. I guess I should have been used to those mind pictures, but I wasn't. As Joanna's image faded away, I tried to fight down the sickening feeling I got whenever I thought about her. It was as if a black balloon stretched inside me, squeezing its way up until it filled my head, blocking out everything else.

Joanna. My mother. How can I tell you about Joanna? If I say that she didn't like me, will you smile and think that all kids feel that way at one time or another? But you see, in this case, it's true. It took me a long time to figure it out. And admit it to myself. What happened that spring only made me certain.

My friends thought it was neat that I got to call my mother by her first name. I didn't. Joanna said the word "mother" made a woman lose her identity. She'd come from a couple of foster homes and didn't really have a mother. She said she'd been a rebel all her life. She met Dad at art school. I think they were hippies. I've seen pictures of them together and they looked like those hippie-types you see on television sometimes. They used to walk in peace marches and go to folk festivals and things like that.

They moved to the country just after I was born. Before that they'd run a silk-screen and print shop with an art gallery in the back. Joanna became an illustrator for kids' books. She was getting lots of work from different publishers. Which gave her a good excuse to pay even less attention to Dad and me.

When I think back, I was angry all the time. Joanna wasn't like any of my friends' mothers. For one thing, she wouldn't let me join the Girl Guides. Or any other club, for that matter. She said it was society's way of herding people together to stifle creativity. That's a bit of a laugh considering she ended up chasing fame and fortune in Toronto. But she was never very consistent. I mean, all I wanted to do was go to Guide camp and learn how to paddle a canoe. She just couldn't see it that way. Yet, when I tried something I thought she'd like, like drawing or painting, she'd lean over my shoulder, shake her head and say something like, "That's not bad, Rachel. But god, it's so ordinary. So dull. Go wild. Use some colours! Let your creative juices flow! Poor Rach." And she'd pat the top of my head and walk away. Subtle, huh? I gave that up, let me tell you.

Most of the time she reminded me of someone with a bad sunburn, so I learned to keep my distance. She'd get mad over lots of little things, but nothing matched her absolute hatred of the farm. She called it either the Dirt Plantation or The Manitoba Gumbo Mud Hole.

One day after school, I walked into the kitchen and faced the inevitable stack of dirty dishes and half-thawed hamburger. I threw my books on the floor, swearing loudly. I'd been cooking meals all week and doing laundry *and* doing my regular chores outside while she sat at her drawing table in the living-room hour after hour working to another publishing deadline. She heard me and

21

made one of her sarcastic remarks, something about "when you live in a mud hole, who needs to keep it clean?"

"If you hate this damn mud hole so damn much, why did you come here in the first place?" I demanded. "All you ever do is bitch about it."

Her eyebrows went up at that one. She looked at me closely and then she smiled a vinegar smile. Lately she hadn't smiled much unless she was going away to see her publishers or to visit friends. Then she could hardly wait to get away. And when she returned, she'd go on and on about her arty friends and all the great places she'd been to. In the last year she'd been away more than she'd been home.

So she turned on the smile and said, "Because, if you must know, it was the thing to do. What can I say? Everyone in those days was moving back to the land, closer to the earth. To *real* life. Huh! What a laugh. Some of our friends moved out here, too. It was supposed to be an artists' colony. But we were all city kids. It was dull here. Gradually everyone moved back to the city. Except us. Your dear father wouldn't budge. It didn't matter what I wanted."

"But you've stayed here for almost sixteen years. How come?"

She gave me a funny look. "My mother ran out on me when I was six. I wasn't going to run out on my kid, no matter . . ." She shrugged. "I wasn't going to be accused of running out when tough times set in, okay?"

I put my hands on my hips. "Tough times? If you love Dad, what's so tough? He likes farming.

You get to do whatever you want to. Why can't you be happy with that?"

I hadn't talked to her like this in a long time, but I'd been having some of my strange dreams. I needed to know.

She slid her water-colour brush through little puddles of red and blue paint. "See these colours? If you mix red and blue, you get a beautiful purple. See? Some people on their own are bright colours. And they blend perfectly with others. But some are like this." She added some green to the red, swirled the brush and the bright colours turned to a muddy brown. "I always thought Alan and I were red and blue. He was so creative. So talented. He moved here so he'd have a bigger studio. That's what he wanted. But he fooled me. He turned green on me in the country air."

"So you and Dad are red and green and together you ended up with brown. The farm. And me," I said bitterly.

She blinked a couple of times and then her eyebrows dipped down as if she'd come to a decision. "If you really want to know, in a way it's true. After you were born we moved out here, and soon he'd stopped painting. He stopped visiting our friends in the city — he just withdrew into a world of cow manure and seed and prairie dirt. A real Manitoba gumbo farmer." I'd heard her call Dad that lots of times. And it always hurt to see the pain in his sun-darkened face.

She looked out the window towards the field. "After you were born, he acted as if you had to

23

be protected from the big bad world. He and I didn't matter any more. Kids do that to some men. Marriage, responsibility, no more hand-to-mouth. End of creativity. Dull. Muddy. Brown. Stability."

I had a feeling she'd wanted to say that to me for a long time. I glared at the side of her face, but she looked down at her drawing. I clenched my hands tight to keep from knocking all her things on the floor.

"So what's keeping you?" I snapped. "Not Dad, right? And certainly not me, any more. I'm almost sixteen. I can look after myself."

Her hand jerked a little when I said that. She dipped a fine brush into white paint, leaned over her work and added a tiny dot in the dark eye of a rabbit in a pink tuxedo.

She blew gently on the white dot and said, "I know you can, Rach." She concentrated on the other eye. "I know you can."

So she was going to leave. That's what she was saying. I'd already had a few of my night dreams about it. Each time, someone different had arrived to take her away with them. And each morning, I'd get dressed, walk down the hall and hesitate at the kitchen door — wondering if it would be empty or would she be sitting there like she did every morning in her terry-towel housecoat, coffee cup in one hand, cigarette in the other, the newspaper propped up in front of her? Whenever I found her sitting there, I was surprised. And then I'd have to struggle with all sorts of feelings. You see, I had to get ready for her going. In the end, my dreams were never wrong.

It finally happened late in June. I bicycled home from school across the back pasture one warm sunshiny day. I walked around the side of the house to find Joanna sitting on a wooden lawn chair, her long legs crossed under a silky skirt, her dark hair caught up with silver combs. She was staring in the direction of the dirt road. Suitcases were scattered around her.

She turned and looked at me, shading her eyes with one hand. "Oh. You're home." She looked back at the road. "Well, you may as well know it. I'm leaving, Rachel. For good. I know you'll be okay here with Alan. I need to get settled before I can really explain things to him. He's out there," and she'd pointed to the fields with their dusty green haze. "Frank will be here soon. He's a friend of mine. He's driving me to the airport. I'm staying with friends in Toronto. You and I'll talk later, Rach. Still, you're better off here. You can look after your dad, right? As you said, you're old enough now."

I didn't answer. I'd heard most of it already in the darkness of my dreams. In the distance, a rise of dust moved along the road towards us. Joanna stood up and waved to the man behind the wheel of a small red car. It crunched over the gravel and lurched to a stop, one wheel sinking into the soil of a small petunia bed. My petunia bed.

"I've got to go, Rach. I'll write." Joanna reached out and fluttered one hand in the air.

"Now, you wait here and say hi to Frank. You'll meet more like him if you come and visit me."

Just like that. If you come and visit. Not *when*. *If*. She was going and she didn't give a damn about me and Dad. Only about Joanna. Always Joanna. When she ran towards the car, I turned and walked away. I took my bike from where it was leaning against the big linden tree and pedalled down the trail through the back wood and out across the east pasture.

Dad and I didn't talk about her afterwards. Not once. This may seem odd, but I was afraid to. Although he went about his regular chores, he had a strange look behind his eyes that scared me. It was as if he'd decided to live without wishing or wanting anything ever again.

To help him out, I took over all the work in the house, doing the laundry, vacuuming the old wood floors and making fish sticks and macaroni and cheese dinners that we ate together in the silence of the big kitchen. It's funny, Dad and I never really talked that much, but we always seemed to know what the other was thinking. I guess that's how I knew that he was really hurting inside. I felt it, a sort of ache somewhere near my heart. Sometimes, when he got up from dinner, he'd lean on the table for support, as if his legs and back had stiffened up. Like he'd suddenly gotten old.

He'd done a few runs in a big diesel truck last winter for a neighbour who'd started a small shipping company. Before I knew it, he'd gone and bought himself his own rig and had taken to the road. For days at a time. And I was stuck on the farm with Mrs. Kimilski from the place down the hill who checked up on me when he was gone. Mrs. Kimilski didn't like kids. But she liked the money Dad gave her, so we got along all right. I thought things would stay that way. Not great, but bearable. What a joke.

One day the farm was ours, the next day it wasn't. He got rid of it. Sold it. And I didn't know why. I just couldn't figure it out. You'd think with Joanna gone, he'd finally get to enjoy the place. I tried to talk to him about it, but he wouldn't stop long enough to listen. Suddenly, he was on the move. Now, he was the gypsy.

Meanwhile, here I was, forced to live in a grungy old house with a bunch of crazy people. It won't be for long, he'd promised. I'll be back, he'd said. He'd deserted me. We could have worked something out. But instead, he'd run away. I sat absolutely still beside Aunt Irene, knowing that if I moved, I'd probably shatter into bits. I hated them. Joanna, Aunt Irene. Even Dad. All of them. I hated them all.

Chapter 4

"Rachel."

Aunt Irene's voice came from a long way off. I tried to ignore it, but she spoke my name again. This time it cut through my thoughts and brought me back to the cold, grey attic.

"Rachel. 'Anger is a weed; hate is the tree.' It can cast a terrible shadow over your life. Your mother is gone, but your father loves you and will come for you soon."

How did she know so much? Had Dad talked to her? Cool fingers reached over and covered mine, but I snatched my hand away. I didn't need anyone's pity. And I didn't need to listen to stupid advice, either.

Aunt Irene shook her head. "Of course. Why should you trust anyone? And as far as that goes, you don't even know me, do you? Even though I've kept a benevolent eye on you and your father, from afar, as it were." She sighed. "I only hope we've done the right thing. Uncertainty makes me quite irritable. I don't like being irritable. It may take some time for both of us to get used to each other. I'm not very good at this, I'll be the first to admit . . . not being a mother myself."

Her fingers grabbed mine and held on tightly. I couldn't pull away without making a big deal of it. Then, to my surprise, my icy fingers grew warmer and I felt a tingling rush move up my arm. Something even stranger followed. My tumbled thoughts seemed to slow down. The bursting anger sifted away and I felt my spine sag. Sighing deeply I closed my eyes. We sat side by side for a few minutes before she said quietly, "Your mother is living in Toronto now, I understand."

I felt a slow bubble of anger rise. She knew *everything*. How? I didn't want to think about Joanna. I opened my eyes and tried to recapture that peaceful feeling again.

"Do you ever hear from Joanna?"

I glanced over at her. She was examining the tips of her lace-up shoes.

"Sometimes she phones," I said in a level voice. "Collect. She says with the number of jobs she has she doesn't have time to write." I didn't bother telling her that Joanna still hadn't asked me to visit. But I remembered. And the bubble of anger burst and spread all through me, prickly and hot.

"Aah, yes, I see," murmured Aunt Irene.

This time I gave a yank and pulled my hand

away. What did she see? How could she see anything?

"I WISH YOU'D GO AWAY!"

I swallowed hard and stared at the floor. Had I said it out loud? The words echoed in my ears.

"Yes," said Aunt Irene lightly. "You're quite right. I must go. I promised Gladys I'd help with dinner, didn't I? She'll be fussing, poor old thing."

I sat very still, trying to sort things out. Didn't I just think those words? I didn't really say them out loud, did I? And yet I must have. She answered, didn't she? I closed my eyes tight. Should I say I was sorry? She was mixing me all up — sharp and unfriendly one minute and nice the next.

"Now, don't you worry about a thing, Rachel. You'll get used to us," she said, patting my arm with a few light taps before standing up and walking to the stairway. She was trying to be cheerful, but I could tell by the stiffness in her voice that she was hurt. "There are two electric heaters set up. You can turn them on. They're quite safe. Dinner will be in one hour. Please be prompt." With that, she disappeared down the stairs.

I fell down onto the comforter. I used to cry all the time, mostly because Joanna made me feel so lonely, even when she was in the house. But, what was the point? This time, though, I almost gave in. Rolling onto my back, I stared at the angled ceiling not far from my head. Two hot tears rolled out of the corners of my eyes. I wasn't crying because I'd hurt her feelings, was I? That would be plain stupid. No . . . no, I was just tired. Tired. Fed up. Cheesed off. Ticked off. Nosy old thing. Bossy cow. That was better. I could feel the anger stirring, and turning, and heating up. Now I was in control again.

I got up and circled the room in search of the heaters. I found one behind a fat dusty chair, the other beside the desk. I turned them both on and kicked off my sneakers.

"One good thing — at least I'm on my own up here," I said out loud, pulling off my wet socks and wiping my nose with one. I held my aching toes near the heating coils. "I should be able to do pretty well anything I want. It will be easy to fool all of them downstairs."

I usually talk out loud to myself when I'm alone. It's a habit I got into when I was little. It helps me think things through. And at that time it also helped to push away those strange thoughts that got tangled up in my brain. Especially the Warnings.

Ever since I can remember, I've had special dreams. I'd dream something over and over again and then sure enough, the dream would happen in real life. Like Joanna's leaving. I never questioned the dreams. And I never talked about them. Joanna would have just laughed at me, or called me a liar. She didn't believe in anything like that.

But the Warnings had started a few weeks after Joanna left for good. For some reason — I didn't know why — I started to see things and hear things and smell things that weren't there. Weird things. Scary things. And not in my dreams.

There was the time I made my math teacher march everyone outside our small school because I'd heard a voice whisper, fire, fire, and had smelled a deep heavy smoke that choked me. The kids and teachers stood outside in the warm June air waiting for the place to go up in flames. It didn't. Not even a puff of smoke.

I'd been teased about it after school, but I knew something was wrong. When I got home I found out that Dad had been fighting a fire at a neighbour's farm all morning. The dense black smoke had swept across the highway and there'd been an accident between a gravel truck and a car. No one died in the accident, but I wasn't surprised there'd been one. I hadn't dared tell my teacher about the screech of brakes and crashing noise I'd heard during the wait outside the school. I was already in enough trouble for sending up a false alarm.

Late in July, I saw Dad's old dog Spark lying limp and wet on the grass outside the barn. I ran up to him, only to have his small body disappear before my eyes. The next day Spark drowned in Hallward's Creek, helping Dad bring in some stray cows during a bad storm. It was the afternoon of old Spark's death that Dad hammered a For Sale sign against the pasture fence. Spark's dying like that scared me. Maybe I was going nuts. What was it like to go nuts? Did people see things before they lost their minds?

I didn't sleep well for ages after that.

When a Warning was on the way, I heard a faint fluttering in my ears or the light around me changed — becoming brighter and clearer. I could sometimes block it if I concentrated on something else, like singing a favourite song loudly over and over again, or reciting the times-tables, or reading a dull history book out loud. School helped sometimes. But sometimes it made me feel even more isolated, because I couldn't tell anyone what I was going through. That's what I wanted more than anything else — just one person who'd tell me I wasn't crazy. You know what? As screwy as all this sounds, there always seemed to be some sort of logic to it. Old Spark *did* die. And there *had* been a fire the day I choked on the smoke in my classroom.

I finally tried to tell Dad about seeing Spark disappear — sort of talking around it, really — but he went positively strange when he realized what I was saying. And I mean strange.

"What? What on earth?" he yelled. "Are you trying to put me on, is that it? Make me feel even worse about the god-damned mess we're in? Is that it, eh?" My Dad never yelled. At least not at me. We were making dinner at the time. I knew he was still really upset about Spark's death, and I guess I should have known better. But I thought at least he'd listen and maybe I'd feel better and maybe he'd offer me some sort of explanation.

Instead, he swung around with a sieve full of wet spaghetti that spewed out all over the floor.

I jumped back out of the way. We stared at each other across the steaming floor. He looked ready to hit me or something

"No, I wasn't trying to make you feel bad," I shouted back. "Jeezz! Forget it. Just forget it! And you can eat *your* dinner off the floor if you want, I'm going to bed!"

And I did. I crept back down later to get a couple of pieces of toast and some milk and lay in bed mumbling to myself, "What do you expect from a Manitoba gumbo, flat-footed, straw-headed farmer. Mud brown! That's him."

I also swore to myself that night that I would never tell another living soul about the fact that I saw things that weren't there. Not ever. I'd keep my mouth shut. I didn't want to end up in a strait-jacket in a mental hospital somewhere.

An even more curious thing happened a few weeks later. When Dad decided to sell the farm he also decided to sell most of the furniture with it. Before he left on a three-day haul, he told me to pack the things I wanted to keep and he'd have them stored. I was to throw away anything I didn't want. I carried boxes and boxes of junk out to our pick-up. Dad was going to dump everything at the local garbage pit when he got back.

I was unloading a carton of old comics when something on the truck caught my eye. It looked like a couple of paintings. Climbing over the mess, I grabbed the string around them, pulled them out and dumped them over the side of the truck. Jumping down, I undid the string and had a look.

One thing was for sure — these weren't Joanna's. Her work was small — mostly wood cuts or water-colours. These were oil paintings. Three of them. They must be Dad's. He claimed he'd burned everything years ago.

Across the first painting was a swirl of dark colours — blues and purples and blacks. Here and there they joined and created little eddies of colour like whirlpools in water. Inside the whirlpools, I saw something that made my scalp prickle — twisted, strange dark faces outlined in black and red dots — men's and women's faces with red staring eyes. I put the painting face down in the dirt. It gave me the creeps.

The second one looked like swirls of smoke — pink and yellow and creamy smoke but the whirlpools were there. In this one, however, the faces of the people were beautiful, pale and sweet, with smiling mouths and laughing eyes. I propped it up against the side of the truck and stared at it for a long time. It made me feel good inside.

The third painting was a self-portrait. Each of the paintings was signed A.M., so I knew Dad was the artist. He'd cut his face in two right down the middle, using the dark colours of the first painting on one side and the softer colours on the other. On the softer side, he'd added one or two rich colours. His dark red hair was as smooth and shiny as a polished hazel-nut and he was young and smiling. The blue eye on this side seemed to glitter with something. I looked closely to see if maybe he'd used a special paint. But he hadn't. In the dark pupil stood a tiny white figure. A little girl. She had red hair. Was it me? I felt my heart stretch and become heavy, with a kind of dull ache.

I tried not to look at the other side, but I couldn't help it. It reminded me of a book we'd read in school called *The Picture of Dorian Gray*. It was as if part of Dad had suddenly grown old — dark and wrinkled and grey. Worse than that, it looked as if he was rotting away. His hair was twisted and swirling and in the little swirls I saw the same dark and dreadful faces of the first painting. The eye on this side looked like the narrowed eye of a wolf.

I didn't know what to do with the paintings. There was something about them, something I couldn't put my finger on, something important. They couldn't end up at the local dump. But one thing was for sure. My father hadn't always been a Manitoba gumbo farmer. Like Joanna had said, he'd been different once.

I'd taken the canvases off the stretcher and rolled them up. They were packed in my big suitcase at the foot of the bed in Aunt Irene's attic. I hadn't talked to Dad about them. I knew he would have burned them for sure. But what did any of that matter now? If he didn't care any more, why should I?

Wrapping the comforter around myself, I curled up in the bigger of the two armchairs. Grey rain ran down the windows under the vines, but the coils of the electric heaters crackled with friendly popping sounds behind their wire guards. The cold air shifted and wavered in front of my eyes.

"Maybe it won't be too bad on my own," I said drowsily. "Maybe everything will calm down — no warnings, no strange dreams, no family, no complications." I snorted softly. Some hope. My toes finally began to warm up.

Chapter 5

"Yoo hoo! Rachel, girlie! Soup's on!"

I woke up with a start. Someone was standing near the desk just behind me. I looked over my shoulder. Nothing. Just the small desk and narrow wooden chair. But hadn't someone just called me? Was I imagining things again?

"Are you there, kiddo? Hop to it and put the feed bag on!"

I wasn't imagining that voice, coming through the crackled wallpaper behind the chair. I noticed a strange metal tube, like the fluted end of a tiny trumpet, sticking out of the peeling roses. I crept up to the hole, my heart beating in my throat. The voice blasted louder this time.

"Hurry up, honey! I'm damn near faint with hunger," shouted Mitzi Dubbles. "We're in the dining-room."

"I'm coming," I shouted down the tube.

"Okey-dokey, honey. Make it snappy!"

I stared at the tube and shook my head. An antique intercom. Things were getting weirder and weirder. Digging around in one of the suitcases, I put on some not-too-clean but dry socks and a crumpled pair of jeans and headed downstairs. When I finally located the dining-room on the main floor — by eliminating a couple of dark rooms that smelled stuffy and cold and edged in mould — I pushed open a set of wide double doors and found myself facing a big round table with a ring of people around it.

Along one wall of the room was a dark sideboard smothered in glass vases and old plates. Across from it stood a monster of a china cabinet stuffed with dusty figurines, smoky glassware and piles of cups and saucers. Strange gloomy landscapes in heavy frames hung around the walls. Very cheerful. Just like the rest of the place.

"Come in, Rachel," snapped Aunt Irene. "You must try and be on time. 'Punctuality is the politeness of kings.' And members of the same household. You may sit there." She pointed to an empty chair beside Luther Dubbles. "Everything gets cold when we wait for the tardy."

"And it tastes worse when it's cold, believe me," said Mitzi. "No offence, Gladys."

"None taken," said Gladys in a soft bright voice. She smiled at me. She'd changed into a rusty green dress of old taffeta. Her skinny arms, like white crumpled silk, hung out of huge puffed sleeves.

"Granny! Why do you take this crap? I mean,

39

letting them talk to you like that! It's pathetic!"

This must be Gladys's twit of a granddaughter that Mitzi had talked about. I looked at her out of the corner of my eye as I edged around the tall chairs and slid between her and Luther Dubbles. She was about twenty-five or so and awfully thin and limp looking — as if there were foam-rubber bones under the dirty blouse she was wearing. She had a narrow pasty face under a fringe of greasy bangs, but she stared at me through a pair of dark eyes as sharp as pins. I looked down at my plate instead. No better. A gooey pile of grey lumps had been slopped in the middle of it.

"Eat up, everyone," said Gladys. "I think it's not too bad at all this time. Of course, Irenie can once again take the credit for saving the day."

"Saving the day?" asked Luther, poking me in the shoulder. "Where did she put it, do you suppose? In a piggy bank? Or did she slide it into one of those night deposits at the bank? I've never been able to save a day. Hard to get in one's wallet."

"Oh you," giggled Gladys.

"Old fools," muttered Greasy Bangs.

"Rachel," interrupted Aunt Irene, "I don't think you've met Mr. Basely."

The man with the yellowing moustache and thinning hair across the table bowed forward over his plate, almost dunking his bow-tie in the grey muck.

"How do you do, Rachel," he said. "I hope you'll be very comfortable here." His voice was deep with a slow even tone that seemed to start

40

low in his chest and come out through his nose. He looked like a retired colonel from a British movie. So tidy. And tweedy. With long pale hands and a long pale nose.

"Mr. Basely came to us when he heard we'd found the house," said Aunt Irene smoothly, nodding graciously in his direction. "A dear friend. The furniture in this room and in the study he brought with him."

"I was an antique dealer," offered Mr. Basely, waving his hand towards the piles of crockery and glassware, but his voice drifted away as he eyed the gooey pile of stew. "I usually like unusual things."

"He often eats out," said Gladys, gazing at Mr. Basely and batting her dusty eyelashes, "and we're so happy he's decided to join us tonight. To meet you, Rachel dear." Bat, bat, bat.

I cringed and looked away. Beside her, Mitzi slowly ate the stew, piling it on small squares of bread. Not a bad idea. I was about to reach for some bread myself, when something snorted against my legs under the table. I froze. Uneasily lifting the table-cloth, I stared down at a pushed-in boxer's face peering up at me through small eyes like pale grey stones.

"Never mind him," said Greasy Bangs with a sneer. "That's Quentin's dog. Filthy slobbering thing. Can't see a thing. Born that way. A freak."

"Who's Quentin?"

"Him over there. Basely. Calls this one Maxwell. If you can imagine. Stupid thing." She gave the dog a sideways swipe with her foot. He grunted.

"Hey, what's your problem! Don't!" I said, pushing her foot away and patting the monster's head. Strings of slobber hung down from the sides of his mouth. He grinned up at me. I grinned back.

"What was that, Rachel?" asked Aunt Irene.

Before I could open my mouth, Greasy Bangs spoke up. "She's just met the damn dog. So now she's met everyone that matters. Everyone except me. But then, I don't count, do I?"

"Of course, you can count," said Luther Dubbles. "Why, I've heard you adding up the money you take from your granny's purse when she's not looking. You've learned to count, make no mistake there."

This guy might look like he'd died twenty years ago, but he was pretty funny. I smothered a laugh by concentrating on buttering my bread with some grainy-looking margarine.

"There's a word for people like you," snarled Greasy Bangs, leaning right across me and pushing her face at Luther. She smelled like sour armpits. I leaned away. "Senile they call it. It means your brains are crumbling away. And then they put you away. For good."

"As long as they pack me in tissue paper and a few moth-balls," said Luther, his skull head nodding. "I'd hate to be put away for good without some care taken."

"Stupid old fart," Greasy Bangs said between her teeth. "I don't know how you can live here, Granny. I really don't. It's no damn wonder you're getting old."

"Better than getting even," said Luther.

"Oh shut up!"

"Now please, that's enough," said Aunt Irene, rapping her plate with her knife. "Rachel, this is Bridgette Snodgrass. Gladys's granddaughter. She's living here until she finds a place of her own. She works at Dawson's bakery down the street."

Instead of saying hi to me, Bridgette snarled back at Aunt Irene. "You said you had no more room. And then you give this kid the attic. I coulda stayed up there. I'm not afraid of some stupid ghost."

I'd been lowering forkfuls of stew to Max, who ate each one delicately off the tines, growling happily to himself. I stopped mid-waist with a loaded fork. "Ghost?"

I felt the hair on my arms lift a little. Had I sensed this ghost? Is that why I'd been so sure that someone was standing by the desk when I woke up?

"Don't be silly, Bridgette. Rachel, she's only teasing you," said Aunt Irene in her sharp voice. "Perhaps you'd be good enough to clear the table, Bridgette. And Rachel will help you bring in the fruit and custard."

"Who was your servant last year, I'd like to know," said Bridgette under her breath — but just loud enough — crashing dishes onto a big wooden tray. "That's me, a bloody slave."

In the kitchen, she slammed the tray down on the table and turned to face me, hands on hips.

"I wasn't kidding around, you know. There's some strange things going on in this dump. And it's all around that room in the attic."

"You said you'd stay up there if you had the chance," I sneered. "How come you'd do that if there's a ghost?"

Bridgette shrugged. "I need a place to stay, that's all. I can't afford some expensive apartment. I have to share with my granny right now. And she sleeps with her mouth open and her teeth out. You should see her. She hardly breathes." She shivered. "After seeing that, anyone could put up with a ghost. That snooty Irene wants me out of here, but I ain't goin' till I'm good and ready!"

A loud rapping on one of the windows made us both jump. Bridgette opened the back door and a small man, wearing blue jeans and a brown leather jacket, sidled in. He had short blond spiked hair, a wide forehead, a pointed chin and narrow yellow eyes — like a smooth-skinned cat. All that was missing were the long whiskers. This time the hairs on my arms wavered around picking up some bad vibrations.

"Roger, honey, you scared the wits out of me," breathed Bridgette, leaning against him. I hoped she didn't start batting her eyelashes like her granny.

He ignored Bridgette as if she simply didn't exist. He was looking at me. But not the way a boy looks at a girl. There was a wary, watchful feeling about him. It was almost as if he was sniffing the air trying to recognize something about me. I felt myself, inside my head, running around slamming doors and tightening the windows making sure I didn't give anything away. He leaned in, looked into my eyes, then he shrugged and smiled — a strange curled smile. "And this is?"

"Her?" said Bridgette. "That's Irene's niece. Rachel somebody or other. They gave her the attic room."

"Oh . . . did they? Staying awhile?" asked Roger. "I thought they might eventually put you up there, Briddie. I was wrong. Not surprised, though. Related to Irene, eh? Lucky you."

This guy was definitely giving me the creeps.

"You've got quite a pile of red hair, don't you? A niece, you say?"

"Sort of," I said. "My last name's MacCaw. Like Irene's."

His cat's eyes widened and he leaned even closer. There was a small dark spot in one of the yellow circles that gave him a funny cross-eyed intense look. This time his lips curled into a smile that seemed a little friendlier. "I guess you'll be going to R.I. Platt Collegiate, eh? Starting tomorrow, I'll bet."

At the very thought of school, my nearly empty stomach lurched.

His smile widened. "Nervous?"

I shrugged. "No big deal."

He grinned, showing small pointed teeth. "Hey, you'll be fine. Quite a crew you've been landed with, huh?" He jerked his head towards the hall door. "Nutty as banana loaves, that lot."

"And I've still got to meet The Ghost in the Attic," I said sarcastically. "That should be fun."

This time he transferred his yellow-eyed stare to Bridgette.

She looked scared. "I never told her about it.

The others must have. I didn't. I didn't tell you, did I, kid? Not me."

The smile tightened on the cat face and the eyes narrowed. I stepped back and tried to look busy with the fruit bowl. Bridgette rushed forward and grabbed his arm.

"Let's go, okay Rog, honey? We'll be late for the movie. The kid here'll carry the dessert into the old farts, won't you, kid? And take the jug of custard in the fridge, okay? You said you would, didn't you? We gotta go, right Rog? The dish pan's under the sink. I'll do the dishes next time, okay? Promise. Okay?"

"Hey!" I called out, but Bridgette had already grabbed her coat off the wooden peg near the door and pushed Roger out into the night. She was about to close the door behind her when her head reappeared.

"Thanks a mill, kid." She looked over her shoulder then back again, lowering her voice. "Sleep tight, eh? Don't let nothin' up top bite, eh?" She snickered and slammed the door.

Chapter 6

I didn't actually see a ghost that first night. It might have been better if I had, because I woke up over and over again, convinced there was someone in the room with me. I got so desperate I even opened my mind to the idea of taking on a "Warning," or even a special dream, but — nothing. A few times, I thought I saw strange shadows flutter along the walls and in and out of the arches. Time after time, I sat up and turned on the lights. Nothing.

Finally, I convinced myself that the new place was making me jumpy. That's all. It would take awhile for me to get used to the light in the attic; the dim glow from the street lamp turned the space into a curiously angled sort of cave.

Determined to keep my eyes open for what was left of the night, I instantly fell asleep. When morning came, throwing its weak watery reflection around the dingy room, I was ready to strangle Bridgette with my bare hands.

I straggled downstairs around eight o'clock to face not only two pieces of burnt toast and black edged rubbery eggs from crazy Gladys, but even worse, the horrible prospect of Aunt Irene walking me to school. Now, I already knew that school would be crummy — new kids, new teachers, new subject problems — but Aunt Irene definitely did not help by standing at the front door in a long fur coat and a wide fur hat telling me that she was escorting me the three blocks to school. *Escorting* me!

I took a deep breath and told her that high-school kids never ever had a grown-up walk them to school and I wasn't about to start a new trend. Escorts were for kindergarteners. Aunt Irene didn't see it at all. She got that set hurt look on her face again. I knew I was going to be overruled if I didn't fight back. I sucked in a fresh load of words, but didn't get a chance to say anything.

Mr. Basely appeared suddenly from the shadowy door of the study and said, "Ah, I see our young woman is on her way to her first day at the collegiate."

"Rachel is refusing to allow me to walk with her," said Aunt Irene through pinched lips. "She's become quite stubborn about it, and we had agreed . . . all of us had agreed . . . as you know — "

"Well now, perhaps she'll allow me to drive her," said Mr. Basely. "I was just on my way to mail some letters." When he smiled, the neatly trimmed moustache below his long nose straightened and bristled. "After all, dear lady, it's raining out there and we don't want you two getting wet, now, do we?"

I nodded rapidly. "That's great, thanks."

Aunt Irene nodded stiffly and one side of her mouth went up. "As you choose. Thank you, Quentin." She turned and walked down the hall without even a goodbye to me.

For some reason, I felt a twinge of guilt. I'd gone and hurt her again, something that didn't seem very hard to do. If only she wasn't so bossy. Somehow when she was around, I felt as if everything I did was wrong — as if she knew all along that I was going to disappoint her . . . and I did. Still, if it got me out of an "escort" to school, that's all that mattered.

I waited on the front veranda and gaped when an old car, as round and shiny as a monster beetle, pulled up at the curb. Great. Just great. Try and act anonymous driving up in that!

I climbed aboard to find Max sitting square in the middle of a folded plaid blanket on the back seat. He blinked his grey stone eyes and growled a slobbery greeting. I leaned over the seat and patted his head.

Even though Mr. Basely drove very slowly, I was glad to see that we'd beat the crowd. The few kids we saw seemed more interested in getting out of the rain than worrying about an almost-hearse purring along under the dripping elms.

I looked at the huge brick school with its front doors set back under a deep stone porch and I wanted to shrink down into my ski jacket. Suddenly I felt very tired.

"Okay?" Mr. Basely asked.

I licked my lips. "Yeah, I'm okay."

"You'll be very careful, won't you? I'll pick you up after school, shall I?" He actually looked worried. "When will that be? Three o'clock?"

I sighed. I'd have to nip this one in the bud. "Look, I'll be walking home, okay? I know the way. Besides, I like walking. I used to ride my bike miles and miles in the country." I felt a wave of homesickness catch me in the throat. I blinked rapidly and stared out the window. "My dad taught me to be careful. Okay? I can handle a few blocks in the city." Who was I trying to convince? Him? Or me.

I waited. Would he get the same hurt look Aunt Irene had put on this morning? He didn't. He sighed and when I glanced over at him, he smiled. Then he looked up and down the street like a cop on stake-out. Just like Aunt Irene had checked over her shoulder in the hallway the night before. Come to think of it, hadn't Mitzi done the same thing before she'd hauled me into the house yesterday? For the first time since I'd arrived, I felt a small whispery flutter in my ears. A Warning was trying to form in that secret part of my mind. I closed my eyes and fought it. One potato, two potato, three potato, four. Five potato, six potato, seven potato, more. I repeated the nonsense verse over and over again quickly. With a faint rustling the Warning drifted away. I opened my eyes. I'd been hoping to get away from them here in the city. I should have known better. Damn. Damn. Damn!

"You're sure you're okay, my dear?"

He looked so worried I said, "I'll be fine. I can handle it. I better go." I opened the door. "And thanks . . . thanks for the ride. I'll see you." I sat on the edge of the seat, hesitating, then stepped down onto the wet road.

He leaned forward and looked up at me through the open door. "We'll expect you home shortly after three. But if anyone, anyone at all, tries to bother you, you must tell us at once. Understood?"

"Yeah . . . okay, I promise. But don't worry. I'm a tough country kid, remember?"

Mr. Basely's smile crinkled and he looked at me right in the eye. "That's what we're counting on, my dear girl. That's exactly what we're counting on."

Chapter 7

The rest of the day was awful. First I had to wander around searching for the room numbers on my timetable. This made me late for most of my classes — which meant I had to face gawking kids and crabby teachers every time I opened a door.

To top the day off, I found I had a locker partner who'd taken up every square inch of space in the tall metal box. I was staring into the jumbled mess inside when someone pushed me aside and said loudly, "Hey! Who's been sleeping in my locker? And where's my lock?"

I held up the combination lock. The tall guy beside me stared at it and then at me.

"Who are *youuu* . . . as the caterpillar said to Alice. *This* is *my* locker." The boy peered down at me. "Explain yourself."

I tried to speak but could only manage a shrug.

I was just too tired. The books in my arms weighed a ton. The boy leaned against the locker door and waited. He had navy blue eyes, prickly brown hair, big ears and a long know-it-all face. Just what I needed. A smart-ass.

"So?" he said. "Are you going to confess, or shall we cut off your head?" He pushed himself away from the locker, bent forward and said in a deep ominous voice, "The principal has a long row of them behind his desk already. Thanks to me."

I ploughed through my notebooks and came up with the white locker card. "Locker 223. Second floor. Combination left 80, right 60, left 22. Right? Well, it's my locker now, too. Okay?"

"I knew it was too good to last," he groaned. "This is just great. I'll have the distinction of being the only guy in school to have an orange chrysanthemum for a locker partner."

"A what?" My voice always squeaks when I'm really mad.

"You mean you haven't seen a chrysanthemum?" He looked up at the ceiling, one long finger resting on his chin. "Let's see. They're a many petalled, large showy flower, often a brightly coloured orange." He looked me over. "It's the hair. Large and showy. And definitely orange."

I knew by the burning flush in my ears that my face was about to run a close second to my petals. "Is that so? Well, you can keep your stupid locker!" I said, pushing my face up towards his. I dropped the lock on the floor and turned away. "I don't think I want to share with someone who looks like Bullwinkle without his antlers. Oh, wait a minute . . ." I stopped and looked the boy's head over. "I'm sorry. Forgive me. I thought those were ears. Antlers, after all." I pushed my way through the crowd.

"Are you telling me I look like a moose?" he called over the heads of the milling students. "Me? The noble king of the Canadian landscape? Thanks, Red."

"Hey!" said a boy, laughing. "Will Bullwinkle. It fits."

Great! Some nosy kids hanging around had been listening. But I was too mad to give a darn.

"God, isn't that just like Will?" said a girl near me. "What a jerk." I threw her a grateful look.

"He's kind of cute though," said her friend. I scowled and continued to push my way through the crowd.

A noise, like the deep trumpeting moan of a sick animal followed me down the hall. Whoever he was, I'd hate him forever. The next day, I carried my jacket and all my books from class to class, telling each teacher that I hadn't been assigned a locker yet. I was explaining this to my new math teacher when I heard a loud snort behind me. It was the tall boy from the locker. He grinned and wiggled his ears with his fingers. Antlers. Definitely antlers.

I bent over my work. The boy's name was Will Lennox, and from the answers he gave in class, he was obviously the math brain. Why do the smart ones always have the biggest mouths? When the bell rang I bolted for the door.

"Hey, Red!"

I ignored him and dodged through the crowd, into the hall.

"Hey, Red! I cleaned out our locker!" he called over the bobbing heads. "Make yourself at home."

I whirled around, but he was moving away through the crowd, hands and books held high above his head. After school I waited until all was clear. When I swung the locker door open, I saw one very small corner had been cleared and in the space lay a large bedraggled bright orange flower.

I looked around. No giggling kids. No grinning big-eared face. I stuffed the flower into my pocket and headed for the nearest exit. This guy was definitely going to be a big problem.

Chapter 8

It rained all that week, the air turning colder. I thought I'd never see the sun again. But I was sleeping better — at least there were no more signs of flutterings in the dark and my dreams must have been boring because I couldn't remember them when I woke up. I'd even convinced Aunt Irene that I could actually find my way to school and back on my own. No way could Mr. Basely have that many letters to mail.

Everything clicked along in the house, well, creaked along, but a few things still bugged me about the place. Bridgette for one. She'd stare at me through half-closed eyes all through dinner and then talk my ear off while we did the dishes. No. Let's get this perfectly clear — I did the dishes — she sat on the edge of the table, swung her legs and talked my ear off. She just loved to describe in detail all the blood-and-gore slasher movies she and Roger went to. Or even worse, get all gooey-eyed and steamy over the TV soaps she and the baker's wife, Mrs. Dawson, soaked up while they slapped icing on cakes and buns.

I didn't trust Bridgette. Not even a little bit. She was too edgy and twitchy, full of stupid eye-rolling and silly smirks, as if she had a secret that had her all tied up in jittery knots. When Roger showed up on movie nights, I got out of the kitchen fast. I hated the way he smarmed around, coming close and watching me with his yellow eyes. The two of them gave me the crawling creeps.

It was a lot harder than I thought to ignore the rest of the crew. I'd started calling them the Fossils. Only to myself, though. As weird as they were, I didn't want to hurt their ancient feelings.

For the first part of the week, they drove me crazy. Wherever I went in the drafty old house, one of the Fossils was right behind me. I couldn't even make a peanut-butter sandwich in the kitchen without one of them popping out of the woodwork.

And were they ever nosy! Especially Mitzi, Luther and Gladys. They asked about Dad, and the farm, and what it was like growing up there — and just about anything else that shot into their heads. Once they even asked me what kind of dreams I had. I got a little suspicious then and asked them why they wanted to know. Gladys said she'd been reading all about dreams in one of the stacks of home-maker's magazines piled up on the kitchen counters. I considered. That sounded like something she'd do. She sure wasn't learning anything from the recipe section. Even so, I kept my mouth shut. I didn't even consider telling them about the Warnings or the dreams.

Whether I liked it or not, I got to know more about them, too. Mitzi and Luther had been in the circus. That fit, in a bizarre sort of way. Mitzi, believe it or not, had been an elephant rider and magician's helper (it had been a small travelling circus — one elephant, three monkeys, that sort of thing), and Luther had doubled as an acrobat and clown. They'd travelled all over Canada in the "good old days" and settled down east when they'd got too old and, in Mitzi's case, too fat to do their jobs any more. There they'd formed a talent agency for out-of-work performers. When that closed down (lack of dedication to the old arts, Luther said), they came to Winnipeg, where Mitzi got a job in a tea-shop reading cards and tea leaves. Luther hired himself out to kids' birthday parties as a clown. But not for long.

"Kids! Miserable little bums. Why, they had battery-operated toys that did more than me," he complained bitterly. "It was me, it seemed, who needed the 'C' cells!"

Sometimes, if the story was a good one, I actually found myself finishing my after-school snack sitting at the big kitchen table. Gladys was always there fussing over her horrible preparations for dinner. Her stories were always sad ones. Like the time she had to give up her house and garden and zoo of stray cats and dogs.

"The city condemned my house," she'd start

out. "They said it was a fire hazard. But it was those neighbours of mine that started it all. They didn't like my little ones. They said my house smelled." She glared at each of us. "*You* tell *me* how one can keep all those little doggies and kitties — and most of them abused, poor little mites — from making the odd error on the carpets now and again."

We all kept our mouths shut. No one was about to tell her that we were glad we hadn't had to live in a fuggy cloud of pee fumes.

Sometimes when she started in on this particular story, I wasn't quick enough to make a getaway. First her chin would start to wobble. That meant crocodile tears weren't far behind. Mitzi always tried to cut it short by saying, "Come on, Gladys, it's all over now, isn't it?" but it never worked.

"Over now? Over now? It will never be over! Not in my mind! My own son, my own flesh and blood turned traitor and signed my life away!" That really got her going — being packed off to a senior citizens' home. This son of hers must have been real slime. What harm was the old thing doing with her dogs and cats? I mean, what difference did it make to anyone else?

She'd run around the kitchen clutching her sweater with one hand and dabbing frantically at the counters with a grubby dishcloth in the other, in a flurry of tidying up. It was almost as if she was trying to wipe away all the terrible memories. Finally she'd wind down and get a dreamy look on her face. "When I first saw Irene, I *knew* she'd come for me. It was fate, of course.

She walked past my room and she *knew* I could help her."

I didn't listen too closely. Half the time she didn't make any sense. Still, I couldn't help wondering why Aunt Irene took Gladys out of the home and moved her to 135 Cambric. Had she simply been sorry for her? But the home must have been full of women just as eager to leave. Why Gladys? She was useless. Couldn't cook worth a darn. Had no money to pay her way. So why? How could Gladys, of all people, help Aunt Irene?

"How come you don't have any pets now?" I asked Gladys once while I was slapping grape jelly on two pieces of toast. "Mr. Basely's got Max."

She leaned forward and whispered, "If I do my job right, then very soon, Irenie says I can have a kitty. Just one, mind you." She held up one crooked finger. "But that's enough for me. I'd like to get a little tabby. Grey with lovely dark stripes. Lovely!"

This reminded me of something that had happened that morning. "Hey. Maybe you could take in that big marmalade cat."

She blinked at me. "Who? Where?"

"He was sitting on the outside window ledge beside my desk, staring in at me through the vines," I said, laughing.

I didn't tell her I'd woken up with the wormy feeling of being watched, certain that the so-called ghost was about to show itself. Instead, I'd seen the flick of a fat tail, and the pointed ears and unblinking stare of a tom-cat. I'd cried out with surprise, and he'd vanished like orange smoke.

Gladys frowned. "I've seen that one. He's after my birds that come to the feeder. I think he's getting fat on them. I don't like that one!"

Her reaction surprised me. I figured she'd take in any stray with open arms. People blow hot and cold over the strangest things.

I hardly noticed, as the days went by, that I was going to my room less and less. I actually found myself looking forward to coming home, knowing that someone was waiting for me. Mitzi even started bringing in her hoard of honey doughnuts and chocolate Wagon Wheels for us to share.

One day, Gladys and I were alone in the kitchen. She was peeling carrots. Over my cocoa, I started thinking about Dad. How long would I end up living here with the Fossils? Would he just decide to leave me here? And where exactly was he, anyway? Aunt Irene didn't seem to know the answer. Whenever I asked her if a call had come through for me, she'd shake her head and lift her shoulders, as if to say, "Isn't that just like a man?" She didn't seem the least bit bothered by it.

In a funny kind of way, that reassured me and worried me at the same time. He must be all right. Otherwise, she'd tell me. Wouldn't she? I couldn't decide whether I was mad at him or worried about him. I was sick and tired of feeling so unsure of everything. I sat forward and clenched my hands. Maybe he'd dumped me, just like Joanna had, but he didn't have the guts to tell me. Sure, he'd promised to return, but maybe it was a big fat lie.

Calm down, I told myself. After all, when had Dad ever given me reason not to trust him? Never. I listened to the scrape and clink of the peeler in Gladys's hand and I wanted to shout, "Then why doesn't he pick up the damn phone somewhere and call me!"

Gladys stopped scraping and looked at me. "Worried about your father, dear?"

I stared at her. "How did you know what I was thinking?"

She smiled her V-shaped smile. "You looked very sad. What else could it have been? Is it because he hasn't called you?"

I nodded, hardly daring to speak.

She rolled up the newspaper and parings in a tight little roll. "I've been wondering that myself. But Irene says . . . well . . . you know what I think? I think he's waiting for you to get settled in. He doesn't want to upset you. He's thinking of you. Don't you think so? That's what I think. After all, it's only been a week and a half, hasn't it?"

I nodded slowly again. Considering it was Gladys, she made a lot of sense.

"Yes, that's right," she continued briskly. "He'll be here before you know it. There now. Carrots done. Meat loaf next. Now where's that new recipe for Italian meat loaf? I'll need six cloves of garlic, I think."

Thoughts of Gladys's meat loaf were enough to drive any other worries out of my mind. I grabbed my books and headed for the door, feeling almost lighthearted. "Er, thanks, Gladys. About Dad, I mean. You could be right."

She smiled brightly and then turned to her recipe, muttering something about chopped black olives and lemon juice. As I walked up the stairs, I decided to give my dad one more week.

Chapter 9

It all started on the way home. I suddenly realized that I was being followed. And by one of the Fossils.

I was waiting at the corner of a busy intersection for the light to change and I happened to look over my shoulder towards the side street I'd just walked along. I noticed someone winding his way through traffic on a bicycle. He was wearing a flat tweedy cap at least three sizes too big. A pair of dark sunglasses hid his eyes. But no one could mistake that skull's head. When I saw him looking back, I waved. He sat up as if he'd been stuck with his own hat pin and wheeled off down a short back lane.

Why didn't he wave? And why was he acting so suspicious, hunching his head down into his shoulders and pulling his cap lower? That's when I remembered Aunt Irene's over-the-shoulder look in the hall, Mitzi's up-and-down street check that first day and Mr. Basely's spy act in the car. Did this mean that after-school question time every day was more than the strange crew at 135 being nosy?

I got another shock a few minutes later when I turned off onto the quiet gloom of Cambric Street. Just ahead, squelching through puddles filled with dead leaves, was a tall loose-limbed boy. Every now and again, he stopped and examined something he picked up in a puddle, replaced it carefully, then continued on his way. It was Will Lennox.

What was he doing walking along Cambric Street? He turned onto the front walk of a tall wooden house with a glassed-in veranda that stood kitty-corner to 135. I waited until he walked across the veranda before scuttling past, making for Aunt Irene's at a fast clip.

"Hey, Red! I thought that was you. Wait up!"

I looked over my shoulder. Will loped towards me, arms and legs flapping like a scarecrow's in the wind. He came to a stop, his hands disappearing into his pockets. The tips of his nose and ears were red with cold.

"So, uh, do you live in this house?" he asked, jerking his head towards 135 and rocking back and forth on his heels. "That's my place over there. Isn't yours full of old people? One of them keeps falling out of trees. Scares the neighbours. Ambulance has been called a half dozen times."

I couldn't help grinning. "That's Luther Dubbles. He worked in a travelling circus. Pretty good, huh?"

Something down the street caught Will's eye. "Speak of the devil," he said out of the corner of his mouth.

"Hello, you young 'uns!" shouted Luther Dubbles, coming at us full tilt down the sidewalk on his bike. "Home already, eh?"

After he'd done a couple of rather stiff wheelies, he stopped and gave us a happy, yellow baring of the teeth. Wisps of hair fluttered around his ears below the rim of the tweed cap. The sunglasses bulged like wasp's eyes. He wore a red and green baseball jacket. He looked like a withered rock star. Or an ancient spy.

"Luther, was that you — " I began but he cut me off.

"A boyfriend already? You shy ones work fast, eh?" he said, looking Will over. He'd already poked me in the arm.

"He's no boyfriend," I said hotly. "His name's Will. He lives across the street. In that house." I pointed.

"Aaah," said Luther. "That boy. We've met your mother, Will. Nice woman. Artist, I believe? Gave us some cookies and a loaf of something when we moved in. Full of green bits. Zucchini, I believe. Terrible . . . terrible . . . but don't tell her that."

Will grinned. "It's all right, sir. We don't tell her what we think of them, either."

Luther positively beamed at him.

This mutual admiration was too much. "Look," I said, backing towards the gate. "I've got homework. I'm going in."

"Not before you help me with my parcels,

you're not," ordered Luther. He lifted two paper bags from the pouches hanging over the back wheel of his bike and handed one to Will and one to me.

The sky darkened suddenly and a faint whiff of rotting leaves on the tail end of a cold, moaning wind blew past us. I looked up at the stark branches of the oaks in time to see an onionskin moon slide out from behind a wall of slate clouds. The house behind us seemed suddenly shadowed and forbidding. I shivered and took a step or two towards Will.

He looked up, too. "Boy. This is like a horror movie or something. Ghosts and goblins and things that go bump, eh? Witches and boiling cauldrons." He threw on arm out. "Oh, come to me, dark shadows of the night!"

Luther whirled to face him. "You watch yourself, young man! It's idle and stupid talk like that that leads to mischief!"

It was the first time I'd seen Luther mad. And he was really mad. Two dark red spots appeared on his thin cheekbones. Right on cue, the wind grew stronger, scattering wet leaves around our feet and groaning in the branches above.

Will nodded and backed away. "Well, sir, I'm sure you're right. And it is getting cold, isn't it? Yes, it is. So, I'll just be running along."

Luther gave me the bag that Will held out — and a shove towards the door — and followed behind, pushing his bike and muttering about young upstarts who think they know everything there is to know when they don't know a blamed thing at all. After chaining his bike, he stomped up the stairs, and almost kicked the front door open. I looked over my shoulder just in time to see Will duck inside his front door. I couldn't help feeling a bit smug. Finally, someone had made him back down.

Once inside 135, I heard the door click shut and the crackle of the paper bag in my arms. I saw Luther put his parcel on the floor and hang his cap on the wooden hat rack. But something . . . something strange was happening to me. A veil of darkness appeared in front of my eyes and began to spin in black whirls. Luther was saying something but his voice seemed to be coming in waves. Was I going to faint? The whirling veil shredded like fine netting and behind it I saw a pale white light. It bobbed and reeled. I gulped dizzily and closed my eyes, but the light floated right behind my eyelids. It grew bigger and bigger, and deep inside its centre, a figure began to form, trying to shape itself, to show itself to me. While it was just a vague silhouette, another dark veil floated between us. Then it too disappeared. I breathed a sigh of relief and opened my eyes. Was it a strange new kind of Warning? What did it mean?

I turned to look at Luther when suddenly, a rushing flap of wings and a long black shadow swooped down on me, flapping and beating the air around my head. I dropped my books and the bag of groceries and covered my head with my arms. I felt a rush of air as the thing passed over me, but almost at once the flapping and beating sounds grew louder again. It was coming back. I crouched lower.

"Rachel, I'm here, take my hand." Luther sounded very close. I reached behind and grabbed him. As soon as I touched his hand, the wings and sweeping shadow were gone.

Kneeling beside me, Luther patted my hand. "There now. Feeling a bit faint, were we? Headache? Cramp?"

Hadn't he seen the bird or whatever it was that had flown over us? For the barest fraction of a second, I saw something else — something that scared me almost as much as those flapping wings and the strange light. Luther's watery eyes had changed, becoming the colour of a winter sky over the prairies, dark and clear. A cold sun burned behind them. At the same time, there was something else, a kind of power surge down my arm and into his hand. I'd felt the same tingling when Aunt Irene held my hand in the attic the first day. Luther smiled as if he'd just seen something wonderful. I pulled away. Was I full of some sort of weird electricity or something? I didn't like this. Who were these strange people? Who was this man looking at me with eyes that seemed to see deep inside my mind? I stood up and backed away.

"Better now, my dear?" he asked. In the dim light, the shadows under his eyes and in the hollows of his cheeks made his face a death's head. But then, he touched the light switch and in the warm glow of the light, he blinked and became Luther again.

I nodded. "Yeah . . . yeah . . . why not?"

"Now, listen old girl, don't let things worry you. It takes time to settle into a new way of life. It doesn't do to rush things. You'll settle in good time." He reached over and patted my arm.

His eyes were pale and clouded and his hand shook a little. Maybe I'd just imagined the electric jolt. Maybe I'd just imagined the change in his eyes. Was I finally going crazy this time? I had to have time to think. I needed to get away from him.

"I'm okay," I said. "I've gotta go. Homework to do."

"That's the ticket," he replied, pressing a crackling package into my hand. "Here. Nothing like red liquorice to sharpen the mind for algebra and great literature."

I turned and ran upstairs. Before I reached the bend in the attic stairs, I knew something else was very wrong. Up there. In my room. I wanted to turn back, but couldn't seem to stop my legs from carrying me all the way to the attic — to what was waiting for me.

Chapter 10

When I saw what had happened in the attic, my heart didn't stop. It bounced straight up and banged around in my throat. Someone had torn the place up. The bed had been turned around, its bedclothes pulled off, and the stripped mattress lay on the floor. The cupboard door stood open. All my clothes were spread around, a pile of them near the opening. I peered into the cupboard. Nothing seemed to be missing. Except . . . ? I groped around. I'd put Dad's paintings in the corner beside the suitcases. They were gone. I ran around, grabbing things off the floor and looking under the few bits of furniture, but I couldn't find them. Someone had taken them. Why?

I walked slowly around the room, staring at the mess, my fists clenched at my sides, my insides lurching. When I passed the door to the storage room, I gave the glass doorknob a twist and to my surprise it opened. Were the paintings in there? I peered inside. A small curtained window offered a glimmer of light. Boxes and covered furniture had been stuffed into the room. Nothing looked disturbed — except for one small box lying on its side. A pile of old magazines had spilled out of it. I poked around a bit, but it was clear that the paintings weren't there. I closed the door on the dust and cobwebs and faced the mess in the attic.

Something was going on in this house. The Fossils were hiding something. From me. Who were they? Why were they always asking questions and following me and keeping tabs on me? Had they done this to the room? What would they have been looking for? The paintings? They didn't have to tear the place apart. It wasn't as if I'd hidden them.

All the fear I'd felt when I first entered the room changed to a deep fury. I began to pace up and down. A scratchy, hot anger was filling my chest and spreading like sharp branches through the rest of my body. I sat down and took a couple of deep breaths.

Maybe *one* of them had done it. Luther? Was this his idea of some sort of joke? No. He wouldn't be that mean. Gladys? Mitzi? It was ridiculous. I just couldn't see one of the Fossils doing this.

But Bridgette would! It could be her way of getting even for not being allowed to have the attic for herself. I ran down the stairs two at a time.

The downstairs parlour was empty. The only sound was the faint muffled ticking of the clock on the fireplace mantel. The dining-room was empty as well. The table was set, but there was no one in sight. Gladys would be in the kitchen. Maybe the others, too. When I swung the door open, I was faced with another empty room. No signs of a smoking dinner. Where was everyone?

In desperation, I even checked out the small larder off the kitchen. I'd seen Gladys come out of there carrying bottles of jams or boxes of quick-cook foods. Turning on the light switch, I saw rows and rows of biscuit and cake mixes, canned meats and tinned fruit. Bunches of dried plants hung from the ceiling. One shelf, across from the door, was lined with funny shaped bottles. Some looked full of slimy, boiled leaves and dark lumps that glistened behind the coloured glass of the bottles. I could almost see the contents sliding around inside.

Other bottles were filled with clear liquids. When I saw the bulging shapes worked in glass on some of them, I grimaced. Snakes were twined around a tall blue bottle, and was that a big beetle on the other? Were these Gladys's? I hoped she didn't get the urge to serve any of that glop for dessert one day when she really got desperate.

There was a small door at the back of the pantry that I hadn't noticed at first. It was painted the same green as the wall. The handle turned easily and the door creaked open. A wooden stairway, the treads painted black, led both upstairs and down into the cellar.

Seeing the stairs reminded me of Mr. Basely's study hidden away under the front staircase. I went back through the kitchen and down the hall. I listened hard at the door. Were they in there? A deathly silence moved in with me under the stairs. Something creaked inside the room. A chair? Someone was coming towards the door with soft padded footsteps. I stepped back and my throat tightened. The door slid open. Mr. Basely smiled down at me, while Max snuffled a soft wet greeting to my knees.

"Why, Rachel," said Mr. Basely. "We were just talking about you. Come in. Come in."

Mr. Basely touched a switch, flooding the small room with yellow light. Around the book-lined space, in a circle of wing-backed chairs, sat the Fossils. They were stretching and blinking in the light. As if they'd just woken up.

"Rachel, dear child," said Gladys, patting the chair beside her. "We were just . . . oh, just . . ."

"Having our regular business meeting. We must talk each week about the upkeep of the house," said Aunt Irene. She held up a slender-stemmed glass filled with a pale golden liquid. "And our weekly glass of sherry. You've caught us out, Rachel."

Mitzi heaved herself out of her chair, walked up to me, gently wrapped soft fingers around my chin and squinted at my face. I had the feeling she was seeing right through me, seeing my pumping heart and shivering bones.

"This kid is upset. Mr. Basely? Irene? Am I right?"

"I'm okay," I said, gruffly.

74

"She *is* upset," said Mr. Basely. "Sit down, child. What's wrong?"

The other Fossils sat forward in their chairs and I could almost feel the air around them quiver as I told them what had happened. When I was finished, they stood up without a word, walked out of the study and trooped upstairs.

"Are you missing anything?" Aunt Irene asked, after everyone had tut-tutted or in Gladys's case moaned and crooned over the mess. I felt like moaning along with her.

"No, I don't think so," I mumbled instead, clenching my hands to keep them from shaking and giving my lie away. I couldn't tell them about the paintings. I'm not sure why, but it seemed important not to.

"What I can't understand," said Aunt Irene, "is why I didn't know this was happening! I'm her aunt! I should have known!"

"Never mind," said Luther. "It's done now."

"But I was just up here, not half an hour before our meeting," said Aunt Irene in her high tight voice. "With some new socks for Rachel. I don't know how your father could let you walk around in those filthy things, I really don't, Rachel. Quite dreadful."

"And her room was all right when you saw it, Irenie?" asked Mitzi.

"Well, I don't know about all right," said Aunt Irene, giving me a sidelong glance that spelled total disapproval. "She hadn't made her bed and her jeans were on the floor, but everything else seemed in order."

I relaxed a little. Talking about things like dirty

socks took the edge off burglars and shadows.

Mr. Basely had been standing looking out of the window near my bed. "Gladys. Do you think you could get Rachel a glass of milk and some cookies?"

"Of course, of course," she cried, running on white sneakered feet towards the stairs. "I'll get some of those chocolate puffs with the jam in the middle."

When she disappeared, Mr. Basely sucked his teeth and said, "Rachel. I've sent Gladys away because I think we should look at the probability that Bridgette is our culprit."

"Oh, I doubt that, Quentin," said Aunt Irene. "I *know* I would have picked that up."

"Irenie, honey," said Mitzi in a slow patient voice, "you didn't even know it was happening when it was happening. None of us did."

"Yes, it must have been Bridgette, Irene," said Mr. Basely firmly. "Who else would it be, eh?" Was that a warning glance at Aunt Irene?

Irene looked at him and shook her head. "I suppose you could be right. Still, you don't think it could be . . . you know . . . he — they, could have found us by now. . . ."

Mitzi cut her off. "For Pete's sakes, Irenie! Of course it was Bridgette. It had to be her. Quentin's right. That dim-wit girl! They don't know we're here. There's been no signs of any kind yet, has there? No, it couldn't be them!"

" 'They'?" I asked.

"May I suggest we clean up this mess," said Mr. Basely, ignoring my question. "May I also suggest that we say nothing to Gladys about our suspicions. It would only distress her. Irene and I can talk to Bridgette on the quiet."

"Good idea," said Luther. "Let's get to work."

"But . . ." I said.

"Never you mind," said Mitzi. "Right now the thing to do is to get this mess cleared up. Okay, kiddo?"

With five people working, it took no time at all to put things right. The last tuck was being put on the bed when quick footsteps patted up the stairs. Gladys rushed into the room.

"Here we are," she breathed in her soft raggedy voice, putting a small tray on the desk. "You know, I hate to admit this, but I have to tell you that I actually thought that my little Bridgette could have snooped around in here and got, you know, a teeny bit carried away. So I phoned the bakery and Mr. Dawson said that he'd dropped Bridgette and his wife off around eleven this morning. To cater a bowling do. Way across town, he said. He's not even picking them up until five or five-thirty. So you see," she said, beaming at the stiff, silent group surrounding her, "it had to be someone else! Isn't that wonderful?"

"Yeah, wonderful," I muttered, looking at the Fossils. "Just wonderful."

Chapter 11

Dinner that night was a dismal event. Knives and forks scraped on the plates, and cups clinked against saucers in the silence of the big dining-room. Bridgette had shown up around six o'clock with a dozen day-old meat pies and then had gone out with Roger. It was great to have a meal without her, but I couldn't seem to taste anything. Not with all those long faces around the table. Even Mitzi left food on her plate. I wanted to believe we were so used to burnt meat and vegetables that we just couldn't taste the bakery pies. But I knew it wasn't true.

After dinner everyone headed for the parlour. Luther offered to teach me how to play dominoes. I didn't really want to be with the Fossils — I kept wondering about them, trying to decide what they were really after. But I wanted to go up to my room even less. So I followed them into the big cold room. Mr. Basely switched on the electric fireplace and we all huddled close to the pathetic puff of warmth off its orange coils.

Luther was a pretty good teacher. I decided I liked the game, but I found myself getting restless. My throat had been a little sore at dinner. Now it was worse and my face felt flushed even in the cold room.

I eyed the Fossils. Aunt Irene was bent over her needlework, Gladys was knitting something long and grey and Mr. Basely was reading a book. Mitzi was solemnly stuffing her face with chocolate snowballs and leafing through *Vogue*. I watched Luther setting up a game, his long fingers moving back and forth. Should I tell him I wasn't feeling well? I didn't want to stir them up again. I was too tired to deal with any more fuss.

Luther cocked his head and said, "I believe we'll have snow tonight."

The others nodded. I looked at the closed curtains with their pattern of fading pink peonies and fat green leaves.

"How do you know it's going to snow?" I asked. "Did the radio say so?"

Luther gave me a slow wink. "I never listen to the radio. Useless things those. I can't do much nowadays it seems, but I'm rarely wrong about the weather."

"But you can't just *know* it's going to snow," I said, feeling fidgety and hot and irritable. "You can't just know something like that. Not unless you get rheumatism attacks or . . . " I stopped. Unless he got Warnings too.

"I have my ways," he said, raising his bony chin and narrowing his eyes. The shadows deepened in his face and for a second I felt something wriggle in the back of my mind. I searched for it, and just when I thought I'd touched it, it was gone.

"Say, are you okay, little one? Still upset about this afternoon?" he asked. "You're looking a little flushed."

"He's right," said Mitzi, popping a coconut-covered ball into her mouth. "Your cheeks are kinda pink, kiddo."

"The inside of my nose is all prickly and my throat's scratchy," I admitted miserably. There. I'd said it.

Aunt Irene dropped her needlework and marched over to feel my forehead. "Hot! She's quite hot. It's started. I just knew it. Didn't I tell you?"

"Started?" I asked. "What has?"

"The flu," said Mr. Basely quickly. "The flu. Your aunt heard from one of the neighbours that there's a bad virus going around. Isn't that right, Irene?"

She nodded. "Yes. Yes, that's right, of course, that's right. The neighbours told me."

"Maybe we should put kiddo here in another room. With you maybe, Irenie," suggested Mitzi. "That room . . . the attic . . . you know."

"No!" I said. No way did I want to share a room with Aunt Irene. "I like the attic. I can see out the window — you know, see the sky and the tree-tops and stuff. And I'm used to the bed now." I didn't look at Aunt Irene. I already knew

80

she'd have that look on her face. Hurt. Why did they make such a big deal about everything?

"I feel she's best up there, as we've already discussed," said Mr. Basely firmly. "We will be vigilant and ready."

"Ready for what?" I demanded. "Look you guys, I—"

"Well, all I can say is this," interrupted Aunt Irene, "Bridgette will have to go. If it was her up there, then she's muddying the waters, so to speak."

"But it couldn't have been my Bridgette," wailed Gladys. "I told you . . ."

"Yes, yes," said Aunt Irene impatiently. "We know what you said."

"We're too trusting by half," said Mitzi, around a bulge in her cheek. She glided up and felt my forehead with a warm, moist hand. "We'll have to be more careful. We thought there wouldn't be any danger until . . ." She was stopped by Mr. Basely clearing his throat noisily.

I was feeling pretty groggy. "Danger? What do you mean?"

Mitzi's Pekinese nose wriggled in thought. These strange birds were definitely up to something. What?

"Well," she continued, "we're trusting old fools, that's all, honey. The day of the open back door is gone."

What was she talking about? They never left their doors open, front or back. There were more locks on this house than in a jail.

"Really, one gets so paranoid," said Aunt Irene. "I mean, we just found the house this summer, how could they . . . he, anyone, have found it already?"

Now what was she going on about? First Mitzi talking about danger. Now, Irene referring to some strange *they* out there looking for this place. I tried to think, but felt too spaced out and dizzy.

"Still," said Mr. Basely, "we have what looks like a young lady with the beginnings of a good old-fashioned bout of flu. She better get to bed. Away you go, my dear."

I stood up and the room took a nosedive. Luckily Mr. Basely was right beside me and grabbed my arm. I steadied. He placed his other hand on the top of my head and looked into my eyes. "We'll take good care of you, my dear. I promise you that."

I felt tears clouding my eyes. I didn't want to cry. It just kind of happened. Slowly and stiffly, he leaned forward and pressed his prickly moustache against my forehead.

"Our tough country girl, eh?"

Mitzi and Aunt Irene left the room in a flurry. Gladys grabbed my other arm and squeezed it.

"I'll take her up to the bathroom and make sure she gargles with salt water." She blinked at me through her pointed glasses, and her chin and nose wobbled. I thought she might burst into tears at any minute. These people were too much. Just too much.

After I'd washed and gargled, Gladys tailed me down the hall. I tried to tell her that I could make it on my own, but she insisted on clutching my arm and half-lifting me up each stair. Mitzi and Aunt Irene were already in the attic sliding hot-water bottles under the covers.

Mitzi straightened up. "You know, Irenie," she puffed, "this really is a sad-sack place to put a kid. Especially a sick kid. Even tidied up it's pretty grim."

Aunt Irene pulled herself to her full height. "Well! I seem to remember pointing that out before she came and I had understood that all of you were in agreement that this would be more than adequate."

"Well, we could give her some decent wallpaper at least," said Mitzi. "Or some of those posters that kids put on their walls. After all, Irenie, you'd met the girl. We hadn't. You should have known she'd need more than this miserable place. We knew beans-all, didn't we?"

Aunt Irene looked so wounded that I blurted out, "I like it the way it is. Honest. It's got everything I need. I really like it."

"We can manage some changes, I'm sure," sniffed Aunt Irene, but her mouth had softened. She even looked a little pleased. "And thank you, dear, that's very nice of you to say." She stared around the room uneasily. "I just hope this is the end of any more nastiness up here. I hope they . . . well. . . ."

" 'They'?" I asked. That word again. "Who are you talking about?"

"Don't you think the child should be in bed?" asked Gladys. "She's shivering. I can feel it." She still had a grip on my arm.

I climbed in and sighed when my feet hit the hot-water bottles. I'd find out tomorrow what was going on. I sneezed. *If* I survived the night.

"Everything all right?" came a reedy voice up the speaking tube. "Safe to come up yet?"

Mitzi bellowed back. "Come on up. She's ready."

"Aaah, here we are, little one," sang Luther, appearing at the top of the stairs holding one of the blue bottles from the store-room — the one with the snakes. "This'll do you right."

"It's okay," I said. "I don't need anything."

The Fossils closed in around the bed. Oh, you must take some, they said. Yes, yes, they echoed each other. It will make you feel so much better, they repeated one after the other.

"But I don't need anything," I insisted.

I looked at Aunt Irene for reassurance. She nodded and actually smiled. "Don't be silly, Rachel. It's quite safe. Luther has a number of home remedies. We all take them. They're quite nice. And they do work."

Luther poured dark liquid into a big spoon. I held my lips tight and thought it over. Gladys reached forward and patted my hand. I opened my mouth and made a face even before I tasted it. To my surprise, it slid down like treacly honey and didn't taste bad at all.

"There now," said Luther, pulling a can of ginger ale out of his sweater pocket. "That wasn't so bad, was it? Drink down this pop with these two aspirins and go to sleep, eh?"

"Luther's elixirs used to sell like hot cakes when we travelled with the circus," said Mitzi, patting my covered feet. "Come on, Luther, let's let the kid get some shut-eye. You too, Gladys. Hop it."

Aunt Irene stayed behind fussing with my covers. I ignored the ginger ale and aspirins. As lousy as I felt, I had to talk to her.

"There's something wrong in this house, isn't there?" I said. "Isn't there? Why do you all talk and act as if someone is after you or something? *Is* someone after you?"

Aunt Irene straightened my covers in a fidgety way, pulling and poking. "Wrong? Don't be silly. You're feverish, dear. What would be wrong?" She tried to laugh but it came out in a coughing sob.

"You can tell me, Aunt Irene. I won't make things difficult. I can keep a secret."

She reached over and brushed my hair off my forehead. Her hand was smooth and cool. Then she turned off my lamp. Her black silhouette stood out against the light coming up the stairwell.

"You needn't worry, Rachel," she said. "You'll be fine. There is nothing for you to bother yourself about, except to get well. We'll take care of the rest. With the five of us, we should be able to handle anything that comes up. Sleep well." She walked to the head of the stairs, hesitated as if about to say something more, and then was gone.

Chapter 12

I lay back on my pillows and studied the glowing heaters. My throat didn't feel quite as swollen as before. It looked like Luther's stuff had helped a little. I tested the rest of my body and decided my joints were still aching but not as badly. But as usual I felt as wound up as a tight ball of twine. Starting with my toes, I slowly relaxed each knotted muscle. It was hopeless. Every one sproinged back into its own little knot.

"Settle down. Settle down," I muttered, punching my pillows into place. "With all of these people around, no one is going to break in tonight. Huh! Unless *they're* the ones who did it. Then I'm not safe from anyone, am I?" I always argue with myself. It helps sort things out. Only this time it wasn't working.

I scrunched down under the covers and pulled a hot-water bottle into my arms. "I think they call that an inside job in mystery books." I shook my head. It seemed hard to believe, considering the way they treated me tonight — kind, concerned, worried. Yeah. Worry was definitely there, all right. But was it just my health they were worried about?

I turned on my side and watched the silhouette of an oak outside slide back and forth across the glass of my window. "Who was it up here this afternoon? One thing is sure — I'm going to find out. I will! I'm tired of letting things always happen to me. This time I'll make things happen."

I grinned into the darkness. "Rachel MacCaw, Girl Investigator. The Fearless Private Eye with the Inquiring Mind. She goes where no girl has gone before." I snorted. "At least my brain is already there — exploring strange new worlds." I yawned loudly.

Talking to myself was making me sleepy. Part of the oak's shadow had spilled over onto the wall by the stair banister. Its twisted branches shifted up and down, moved by the night air. My eyelids were growing heavy, when another shadow, a different one, flitted across the wall between the etched pattern of branches.

My eyes popped open. What was that? The strange shadow flickered back across the wall. Was it coming up the stairs? Was it going down? Was it the winged shadow that had attacked me in the hall? What should I do? Should I call for help? Call who? Could it be one of the Fossils creeping around in my room?

Slowly and deliberately, I reached over and

turned on my bedside lamp. There was no one in the room. My head felt fuzzy and a dull pain had started in the back of my neck. Reaching for the aspirins, I worked them down my tight throat with a gulp of ginger ale and some silent gagging.

I fell back on my pillows. "This is stupid. I've got to get to sleep and I can't sleep with this dumb light on," I said fiercely. "There is no one here. There is *no one here.*" I rolled over and turned off the light.

The room had no sooner dropped into darkness than the strange shadow fluttered across the wall again. Sitting up, I peered through the window. Maybe something out there was doing it. To the right I could see the street lamp, the silent road on the other side of the lilac bushes, and not far away, a slice of Will Lennox's house. Could that room in their house, the one with the light still on, be Will's? Was he awake, too? Thinking about Will and his big ears made me think of school. As much as I hated moving to a new school, at least there, in the noise and confusion, things seemed normal . . . uncomplicated. I actually found myself looking forward to going back, flu or no flu.

A cold wind outside sifted between the cracks in the window casing and through my pyjamas. Climbing back into bed, feet against one hot-water bottle, arms wrapped around the other, I finally drifted into a headache-y exhausted sleep.

I don't know what time I woke up. One minute I was fast asleep and the next I was wide awake — tense, alert. The room was so quiet I could hear, like a whisper in the air, the faint whistle of the wind outside and the gentle rumble of cars on distant streets.

Even before I turned my head, I knew that someone was in the room with me. I fumbled for my glasses and put them on. Looking towards the centre of the room, I saw something I knew I shouldn't believe — a strange luminous vapour was forming in the air near my desk. It began to turn in and around itself, like thick smoke from a camp-fire. The glowing light inside it grew larger and brighter until the heaters' orange lights faded next to it.

The vapour continued to turn, like a slowly spinning funnel and began to take on a shape. The funnel slowed almost to a stop. A shimmering hand with long fragile fingers reached out. The hand touched the top of the desk and traced the back of the chair with what seemed like a sad, aimless gesture, the fingers slowly sliding over each object. This had to be Bridgette's ghost!

The hand was followed by the rest of the figure. My breath caught in my throat. I swallowed the horrible tickling back down, trying not to cough and give myself away. The lighted figure began to drift slowly across the room towards the window under the arch that faced the front street. Any second now it would be out of sight behind a jutting wall.

Which would be worse — getting up and keeping track of it or waiting until it drifted back into sight, maybe right beside my bed? That last thought was enough for me. I sat up and coughed — dry, hacking sounds in the silent room. When I opened my watering eyes, I saw the glowing head turn and look straight at me.

I put my hands to my lips and gulped hard. The figure's shoulders and body turned and began to follow its gaze. "Who are you?" I croaked.

It was close enough now for me to see some shape to the face — shadowy eye sockets, a narrow chin and high cheekbones. It raised one long silvery hand. I was certain it was going to say something. I might have been able to sit still if that was all, but it began to glide closer and closer. I guess I panicked. Groping through the darkness, I grabbed my lamp and turned the switch.

I expected the figure to vanish in the light and it did. But not right away. Standing in front of me was a pale young man, wearing a long old-fashioned housecoat and brown slippers. His eyes remained deeply shadowed, but the mouth was full-lipped and the chin firm. The rest of his face was very thin, as if the flesh had wasted away. He was leaning towards me, one hand held up, as if asking me to wait. Then, he covered his eyes with his arm, turning away from the light. He began to fade quickly.

Something about this last movement told me not to be afraid. I turned off the light. But it was too late. The black silence vibrated through the arches of the old room. He was gone.

Chapter 13

I woke up the next morning curled like a snail on the end of my bed. The light in the attic was different than other mornings; it glared off the ceiling instead of creeping in slowly over the window sills. Putting on my glasses, I leaned close to the window and peered out.

A spreading white world stretched across the street and road and yards nearby. The lilac bushes that edged the yard were huge cottonballs. Each branch of the old oak had its own woolly muff. A car lumbered along the front road, kicking up silent clods of snow. So Luther had been right. He said it would snow. And it did. If he could do things like that, maybe the other Fossils could, too. I sighed. I usually love the first snowfall, but thinking about the Fossils took away the pleasure of it — especially thinking stupid, wild thoughts. And something else was niggling at me.

I rested my arms on the window sill and frowned, trying to remember. Then it burst into my mind — a picture of the dazzling figure from the night before. That did it. I swallowed hard and a fiery pain cut into my throat.

"Ugh! That hurts," I croaked, crawling under the covers and searching for the barely tepid water bottles. The covers were twisted, and after I'd straightened everything out I felt hot and sick. "It must have been a fever dream," I decided. "Or just another sign that my brain is scrambled. Maybe it'll turn to mush soon and I'll be no good to anyone." I yawned hard and wide. It was too late. My brain already was mush. I turned over and went back to sleep.

When I woke up again, the sun slanting into the room had a yellow afternoon warmth to it. I sat up and scrubbed my fingers through my hair.

"I did *not* dream that ghost. He was as real as this bed I'm sitting on. What am I going to do? I can't tell the Fossils. I just don't trust them. Something really weird is happening here and I am definitely going to find out what! Just as soon as I can sit up longer than two seconds without feeling as if my aching head is going to drop off and bounce across the floor," I added, as I lowered the poor thing back onto the pillows. A few minutes later, Aunt Irene appeared with a breakfast tray.

"It's lunch, actually," she said, putting it on my lap. "I had to throw away two poached eggs earlier. Luther was up here and said you were still sound asleep, so we waited to feed you."

She made it sound like they were keeping an animal in a zoo. On the tray was a plain boiled egg, a huge glass of fresh orange juice and a couple of Gladys's scones. I knew if I dropped one of those rocks, it would probably go right through the floor and hit some poor unsuspecting Fossil on the head. I eyed Aunt Irene over the rim of the juice glass. She was staring around, uneasily adjusting the cuffs of her sweater over and over again.

"You okay?" I asked.

She looked at me startled. "What, dear? No! I mean, yes, I'm fine. Did you see the snow? It must be two feet deep out there. Also, some boy from your school called. I told him you weren't well." Her eyes darted here and there. "You needn't worry. About anything. You'll be all right, of course. We're here to settle any problems. Mitzi agrees. But she knows only up to a point, naturally. That's the problem. Only up to a point. After that . . . " She stopped suddenly, looking guilty. "I'm rambling. Soon I'll be as scatterbrained as Gladys."

I sat up. My brain swooshed to one side. "Look, what is going on around here?" I demanded. "You're worried about something. Why can't you tell me what it is? Why is everyone talking in riddles? What's the big secret?"

Aunt Irene fussed with the covers. "It's only that you're in my care, and I want everything to go nicely for you. I want you to . . . well . . . to have time to settle in with us. And I don't

93

want to upset your father. He called earlier, by the way. But I didn't want to wake you."

"Dad? He called? When will he call back? What did he say?"

"He said he was going to be on the road all day and night. He got another load to take up north somewhere in Alberta. I told him not to worry."

"But I have to talk to him! I have to!" I cried.

"He said he'd call back soon. I must get downstairs," said Aunt Irene, in a soothing voice. "We have another tenants' meeting. A new furnace this time. If it isn't one thing, it's another. Give me your water bottles and I'll get Bridgette to fill them and bring them back up."

"Aunt Irene," I said slowly and evenly. "I want you to tell me why you are all so worried. Are you expecting someone to break into the house? Or has he already broken in? In my room? Why can't you tell me?"

She jumped as if I'd poked her in the side. "Tell you? There's nothing to tell you, dear. Not right now. We . . . we . . . " She tugged at my covers with little jerks and pulls, straightening them over and over again. "I've already said, don't you worry about a thing. We've already talked to Bridgette about her little escapade up here."

"But you know she didn't . . ."

"Now, I'll be up later, and we'll talk some more," she said, disappearing down the stairs with a little wave.

"I just love our little chats, Auntie!" I shouted to the empty room. "I just love knowing nothing about what is going on in this NUT house!" I clutched my throat. Shouting hadn't done it any good, but it had helped my spirits no end. I snuggled down under the covers and began plotting.

I had barely got started when heavy footsteps came up the stairs. Now what? Bridgette's greasy head appeared, followed by a grubby pile of sweaters over droopy polyester slacks that bagged at the knees. On her feet were a pair of slippers shaped like pink pigs' faces. They slopped across the wooden floor towards me, their toy eyes wobbling.

"This bloody place is bloody freezing," snarled their owner. "Probably freeze up your veins if you didn't keep moving. Stupid furnace is broken. We've only got two hot-water bottles and the Queen of the Dump says you get them. Here." She threw them on the bed.

"Gee, thanks," I said sweetly. "Hope you didn't strain yourself."

"Hey, don't get mouthy with me, okay? 'Cause I came up here to tell *you* off good and proper." She glared at me through slitted eyes. "I hear you told them I was messing around in your room. In the little princess's tower, eh?" She put her hands on her hips and pushed her chin out.

I sat up. "No, I didn't! Someone was up here yesterday and they tore the place apart. I didn't say it was you."

"Yeah, well it wasn't me up here okay?" She brushed her hair out of her eyes with a bony hand. "I was at work and I can prove it." She

95

leaned over me and I could smell her sour breath. "And it wasn't Roger, neither. What would he want up here? Nothin'. That's what!"

Roger? Why would she bring up Roger? "Oh, yeah? Well, I didn't . . ."

"Yeah? Yeah? Well, remember this, kid," Bridgette mimicked, her face inches from mine. "Don't go blabbing about nothin' to nobody, if you know what's good for you. And I ain't kidding." The pigs' heads slapped across the floor and down the stairs.

"How could I blab anything to anyone in this place? No one wants to hear what I have to say," I shouted. My sore throat squeaked at the end. "No one."

Chapter 14

The Fossils must know about the ghost, I decided. But why would they put me up in a room that had a ghost hiding in the woodwork? Did they want me to see him?

I was sitting cross-legged, my chin resting on my hand. "Why? Why? Why?" I muttered. "If they know about the ghost, they must be wondering if I've met him. They're usually so full of questions, and now, when they have a chance for a good one, they don't ask. So now what?" I shook my head to clear it and reached for the hot-water bottles.

Typical. Just like Bridgette to put lukewarm water in them. I shoved them under the covers just as someone bounded up the stairs.

"Hi! Hear you've been sick. Mrs. Dubbles says you could use cheering up. She told Mr. Dubbles you need to know there's an ordinary life out there. I guess that's me. Ordinary."

It was Will Lennox. I held the covers up to my chin and searched around on my bedside table for my hairbrush. It was in the bathroom downstairs. I grabbed a tissue instead and wiped my nose vigorously. I couldn't believe it. Why had those stupid people let *him* up? Will lounged up to the bed, squeezed past it and sat on the window sill. "Jeez, you look like death warmed over. Or maybe I should say death cooled over. This place is freezing."

I sneezed into the tissue and looked at him with watery eyes. "What are you doing here? And how did you get past them?"

"I can see how thrilled you are, Red. But . . ." He stopped and grinned. "I'm here out of intense, burning curiosity. I couldn't wait."

"Oh? Wha — " I sneezed again and grabbed another tissue.

He held one knee between his laced fingers. "Well, I'll tell you. I couldn't sleep last night. I have this chair beside my window that I sit on when I can't sleep. I do my homework there, and sometimes I eat there, and. . . ."

"Get on with it. I've got some serious decision making to do today," I snarled. "I don't have time for stupid games!"

"My, my, aren't we cranky?" He looked around the attic with interest. "Neat place. So . . . anyways, I think it was about one a.m. when I woke up. I knew right away I was having one of my wide awake times. So . . . I sat in said chair and looked out said window. I get quite a few of these wide awake nights. They're not too bad, except . . ."

I waited, every nerve in my body still.

". . . well, I get kind of lonely. It seems almost — "

I jumped in impatiently. "Tell me what you saw out of *said window* or I'll throw one of Gladys's rock scones at you. It could be painful."

Will twisted his lips to one side, frowned, then wiggled his eyebrows up and down. "Mmmm. Well . . . I may as well come to the point."

"Good idea."

"Okay. You asked for it. Just don't laugh."

"I won't laugh. I'll take aim, though, if you don't get on with it!"

"Okay, okay. I saw something . . . a weird light moving around this room. I would have figured it was you, except I'd already seen it a couple of times. Before you came, that is. The first time I saw it, I thought it was a flashlight. But it wasn't directed like a beam. And it was a funny bluish-white colour. And last night, I finally got a better look at it through my binoculars. It came real close to that pointy window that faces the street. Even though there are vines across it, I could have sworn it was — you're going to think I'm nuts . . ."

I licked my lips. He'd seen it. I wasn't crazy! "Get on with it," I managed to say.

"Well, it looked like a person — a person surrounded by a hundred sparklers. Hey! You saw it, too. I can tell. You just turned the colour of Elmer's Glue."

All I could do was nod.

"You did?" He leaned forward. "How about that! Then I wasn't seeing things, after all. Thought I was going nuts. What was it?"

"A ghost."

There. I'd said it. I'd actually said it. Let him sit there with his mouth hanging open. At least I'd found something that could shut him up.

Not for long, though. He stared for only a second before jumping up and shouting, "A ghost?"

"Shut up! Keep your voice down. They'll hear us."

"A ghost!" he whispered loudly, the cords on his neck standing out. "That's incredible. I knew it! But of what? A ghost of who?"

"I don't know."

"So what happened? Did it talk to you? Make any sounds? I can't believe it! What did it look like? And you had one right here! Did it moan or knock three times on the wall or anything?"

I eyed him. "What makes you think I'm not lying through my teeth?"

He sat back and spoke in a normal voice. "Are you?"

"No. I saw it all right."

"So what happened? Tell me exactly." He settled himself on the window ledge. "Red, I'll keep this to myself, I promise."

"Why should I tell you anything?" I said harshly. "So you can make fun of me? Why are you here, really? Did they send you up here to grill me?" I knew I was being awful, but I couldn't help myself. "I wouldn't put it past

100

them. Or are you just being nosy — big joke and all that, eh?"

He stood up. "Hey. I'm not into being nosy, okay? I thought you might like someone to talk to. I came over, first of all to tell you what I saw, then when they told me this was your room — in the attic — I got worried. They weren't going to let me up. But I talked a blue streak and they gave in. Gladys likes me. So does the fat one — Mrs. Dubbles."

"Mitzi isn't fat," I snarled.

"No? You coulda fooled me."

I sighed. "What do you want? A good story that you can pass on to a couple hundred of your closest friends at school? Page one — An Encounter with a Teenage Lunatic?"

"Jeez, you are really a scratchy one. I can live without your mouth, you know? I can also live without knowing about your stupid ghost, too. I have a purely scientific curiosity about it, that's all. But don't come to me when he tries to drag you down into the great beyond or something." He pushed his way along the bed and headed for the stairs.

I waited until he put his foot on the first stair before blurting out, "If I tell you what happened will you promise on a stack of bibles that you'll keep it an absolute secret?"

He turned and looked at me. "How big a stack?"

"You know what I mean. Will you?"

He nodded. "But only if you promise on the same stack that you'll believe me when I say I won't. Tell, that is."

I looked out of the window and thought. "Okay. I'll try to trust you."

"Not just try. Trust."

I looked at him. His big ears were flushed, his hair stood on end, but his eyes were dark and earnest. I had to trust someone. Maybe now was the time to take the chance.

"And I'll tell you something else," he continued. "I don't have a really close friend, let alone a couple of hundred. Some of the kids think . . . well, I'm kind of . . . weird. But I don't care. I'm going to be a famous scientist someday. They don't take their school work seriously enough, you know? They're all just bored to death, and . . ." He glanced at me and shrugged. ". . . my brain just keeps revving — like my mouth. I try to keep it shut, but it just sort of takes over sometimes. My dad says I've got to be more tolerant."

I nodded in agreement.

"So what happened last night?" he asked in a soft sad voice. Maybe I shouldn't have nodded.

It took me a few minutes to sort out the mess my mind was in. And even longer to tell him because he *would* keep interrupting. I told him about the Fossils and their weird behaviour, I told him about the break-in, about Bridgette and finally about the ghost in the room the night before. I kept the Warnings and the winged shadow to myself. I figured I'd told him more than enough for one person to swallow all in one go, no matter how eager that person seemed to gobble down more.

When I was done, he rubbed his nose. "Sounds to me like the wrinklies are eager to have you here, but really worried about something."

"Yeah. They're worried about *him*."

"Him? Who?"

"*Him*. That's what they call whoever it is they're worried about. Sometimes they change it to *them*."

"That makes a lot of sense," he said, sarcastically.

"Well, that's what they say, okay?" I said. "Things like, 'It can't be *them* doing this,' or 'How could *he* have found the house already?' or '*He* doesn't know we're here.'"

"So who is this *him* they're talking about? The burglar? Or the ghost, maybe? What do you think? And who are *them*? Bad guys? More ghosts?"

"How should I know? I just moved in. Remember?"

"But more importantly," Will said, ominously, "*who are those old people downstairs?*"

I sat up. "What's that supposed to mean? They're my great-aunt and her friends. My Aunt Irene is my dad's aunt."

"How do you know that for sure? You just finished telling me that she and Mr. and Mrs. Dubbles and Mr. Basely were down east for years and years."

I chewed my lip. "I don't know absolutely, for sure. But my dad knew it was her."

"Aaah, but how well did your dad know her

before she came to visit you, eh? Maybe she's just pretending to be your aunt, and he saw no reason not to believe her."

I shook my head. "I don't know about the others, but I'm pretty sure she's my great-aunt. After she visited the farm I dug through some old family pictures. I was sorting stuff out before we moved. She was in a few of the photos, all right. She's a lot older now, but it was her. It has to be her!"

"Okay, okay, keep your red hair on. So, let's assume that she's your aunt. Who are these other geezers? Where did they come from? And what connection do they have to the ghost?"

"Who, what, where! I don't like riddles! I've never liked riddles!" I said, angrily. "Look, let's forget it. We were probably both seeing things last night — "

He waved his hand in front of my face. "Never mind that kind of talk. Just tell me what you really think of your aunt and the wrinklies."

He'd never give up. I fell back on my pillows and pulled the covers over my head. How did I feel about them? Good question. How did I feel about nutty old Gladys and her burnt suppers, Mr. Basely and his kind voice and pepperminty manners, Luther and his acrobatics and medicines and spying, Mitzi and her chocolate breath and warm bossy ways? And what about Aunt Irene? She was the hardest to figure out with her starchy temper and her hurt looks.

"Hey! Are you asleep? I need answers up here."

I stuck my head out. "Okay. I can't believe

I'm going to say this, but — if you really want to know — I think I almost like them. And I think they like me, too. I *think*. Most of the time, anyway, but then sometimes they act different . . . strange . . . almost as if they're sorry I'm here — as if they aren't who they seem any more. It gives me the creeps, you know? Like when they were sitting in the dark in Mr. Basely's study. I know they weren't talking. If they'd been talking I would have heard them. When the lights came on, it was like they'd come out of a trance or something. And they're always hanging around asking questions. But it's like they already know the answers."

"I see what you mean. They interrogated me for ages before I could set foot up here. I think they're up to something all right," Will said. "Bad or good, I don't know."

I felt the familiar wriggle of fear in my stomach. "Great. And I'm stuck here," I said. I smacked my hand down on the covers. "I'll tell you one thing. I am definitely going to find out what they really want!"

Will chewed on the side of a fingernail and examined the result before answering. "The way I see it, they would have done something to you by now if they were a bunch of psychos. Which I'm sure they're not, so don't go crazy. Secondly, if they were going to do something to you, they wouldn't have registered you at school or let you talk to me. So. . . ."

"So what?" Now it was my turn to convince him. "What about the ghost? I'm absolutely positive that Aunt Irene knows about him. You should have seen her up here a while ago. She practically tied her fingers in knots looking all around the room. As if she expected a firecracker to go off under her backside or something. And if she knows, the others know. Believe me!" My head had started to ache again. I lay back on the cool pillows.

"Okay. Now. If you're right, this says a lot. So, let's think this through logically, as Spock would say. One. They are up to something down there. Right?"

"I guess." I closed my eyes and felt myself sink into a tired sort of despair.

"Two," Will continued, undaunted. "They know about the ghost up here. Right?"

"Yeah . . . I think so," I murmured.

"Three. The ghost must be connected to them somehow. Correct?"

I opened my eyes. "Not necessarily. They might just know about it from the people who owned the place before them."

"Boy, when you think logically, you aren't very sure about anything, are you?" he said, shaking his head.

"*You're* the one thinking logically, not me," I sneered, then stopped short. "I mean, you *think* you're thinking logically. I always think logically."

"Sure, you do, Red. Sure you do. But let's get this part clear, at least. You do believe there is a ghost, and that they know about it. Correct?"

"Yes. Yes. Yes! Now, you sound as if you don't believe it."

"Cool it. I believe. I believe. But don't you

see? You're telling me they put you up here knowing there's a ghost that likes to light itself up at night. Why? There has to be a reason."

"I don't know," I moaned. "I can't think. I don't want to think any more!"

"Listen — no, listen," he said, waving me quiet. "After seeing that strange light the first time, I looked up ghosts and things in the library. For instance, do you know what poltergeists are?"

"I'd rather not." I shivered again and looked for shadows fluttering along the walls.

"Very clever. Now . . . poltergeists chuck things around and they seem to show up when there's a kid nearby. They use the kid's energy somehow. You know, for throwing books and dishes around and stuff. So, maybe you're the kid this ghost needed — hey!"

"Now what!"

"That's it! Maybe they're ghost hunters. The wrinklies, I mean. There are such groups. I read about them."

"Get serious," I shot back. "The Fossils bought this house and they almost never leave it."

Will opened his mouth, closed it, blinked a few times and opened it again to say, "We sure are scientific and logical, aren't we? Ghost hunters . . . what do you suppose they carry? Phantom film in their cameras? Do they leave out spiked angel cake for the ghosties and ghoulies? Do they use ghost nets? A little hard to pin them down, I'll bet, huh?"

We looked at each other and grinned, then burst out laughing.

"Will you please get serious?" I said, gasping for air.

"How do you know I'm not?" he asked. "Do you know how to catch a ghost?"

"No," I grinned, "and neither do you."

"Point taken. In any case, there has to be something special about this house. About this particular ghost. And there has to be a link with your aunt and the others." He sat back. "Now, that's logical."

I thought this over and nodded. "They do talk about 'finding the house.' As if it's something special. And they seem to be waiting for something really big to happen."

"You said they were expecting someone else to move in, right?"

"Yeah, to stay in the empty bedroom downstairs."

"Mmmm. I wonder who it'll be?" He shook his head. "You know, it could be that they invented this mysterious person as a way of putting you up here with the ghost. So they wouldn't have to explain why you didn't get the empty bedroom."

"I hadn't thought of that," I said.

"What we need to do is find out more about this place." He looked at his watch. "You know what? It's four-thirty. My dad should be home. He might know something about it. He's doing a photo book on old houses in Winnipeg, so he's doing a lot of research. I'll ask him."

I thought about it. "No," I said. "I'd like to be there when and if you ask him. I don't want to hear anything second hand."

He nodded. "Tell you what. When you're feeling better, I'll take you across to see him. He loves to talk about his old houses. Meanwhile, maybe you should ask for that other room."

"They wouldn't let me have it. I'm stuck here. I know it."

"So sleep on the living-room couch. I could loan you a sleeping bag. You could sneak down at night."

I shook my head. "I'm not really afraid of the ghost. When he looked at me, he looked worried. I know he wanted to talk to me."

"Jeez, are you sure?"

"I'm sure. At least now, I'm sure. When it gets dark there may be a whole new view on how brave I am. I'll take the chance. And if it gets rough I'll run downstairs." I yawned. "Look, you'd better go, I — " Suddenly, near the desk, something hit the floor with a bang. We turned and stared. A puff of dust rose out from under a book lying in a shaft of sunlight on the floor. I looked at Will. His eyes were bulging. Just then, another book skittered across the desk and fell to the floor with a loud slap.

Will's lips barely moved. "I think someone else is here. I think we're being told something," he said in a quiet sing-song voice.

I nodded, the back of my stiff neck almost squeaking. We sat without moving for what seemed like hours. When nothing else happened, we both exhaled loudly.

"Did you put your books on the edge of the desk?" Will asked in an accusing voice. "So they could fall on the floor?"

"Of course not! And even if I did, how did I get them to fall on either side of the desk? I stack all my books along the wall between a pair of brass bulldogs Aunt Irene gave me. Book-ends."

Will crept towards the desk, looking like a long-legged spider creeping up on a dozing fly. He stared at the books, leaned close, straightened up and said, "What you're saying is that these books fell from between these heavy book-ends at the back of the desk onto the floor on either side of the desk."

"That's what I'm saying. Logical enough for you?"

He hurried back to the bed and sat on the edge of it. "You know what I think?"

"I'm afraid to ask," I sighed.

"I think we now know who might have tossed your room." He pointed in the general direction of the desk. "Ghosts do that."

"Oh great. Now I'll have things flying around my head all day and night." I held my hands over my ears and closed my eyes. "I'm going to go stark raving nuts. Why can't everyone leave me alone!"

Will bounced up and down on the bed until I opened my eyes. "Go nuts later. Right now, we've got to approach this in a scientific . . . in a logical way like —"

"If you say like Spock, I'll smash your teeth in " I snarled, but I had to laugh at the look on his face.

He grinned. "You are so touchy."

"How can you be so . . . so excited about all this?" I'd lived so long with this sick feeling in my stomach that it was hard to believe that someone actually was eager to throw himself into the centre of something that he didn't understand.

"It's the chance of a lifetime! A real live ghost . . . well dead ghost, I guess . . . but a *real* ghost to investigate. Aren't you curious? Aren't you intrigued? This is a chance to really explore something that can't be explained away. You know?"

I put my chin on my knees. "I guess I do. It's crazy, but I know I'm not going to leave here without finding out what this . . . this whatever it is, is all about."

"Good! Tonight I'll stay awake. And as soon as I see anything even remotely like the light I saw last night, I'll be over here in a flash. With camera in hand. And no phantom film, either."

"Hammering on the back door and waking everyone?" I said. "Good idea."

"Mmm. Yes, a slight technical problem." He thought a moment. "Let's do it this way. I'll be over at the stroke of midnight. You let me in the back door. We'll sit up here in those old chairs for a few hours. If nothing happens . . . ghost-wise, that is," he leered at me, then held up his hands when I glared at him, "just kidding, just kidding . . . if nothing ghostly appears, then we try tomorrow and the next night and the next until Mr. Iridescence shows up. Whaddya say?"

His eyes were bright. He was grinning from ear to ear. I glowered at him. Nice for him. He didn't get Warnings. He didn't get a dark flapping shadow swooping over his head, either.

111

"I'm glad someone can joke about this," I blurted out. It made me mad to see him so darn proud of himself. "Well, it's not a big adventure for me, okay? You weren't dumped by your father onto a bunch of very weird people, were you? You didn't see a ghost float up beside your bed, did you? He didn't look *you* right in the eye, did he?" I was trembling as if a chill had washed through my whole body. My headache had come back, dull and heavy.

He looked as if I'd hit him on the back of the head with a big stick. "Jeez. Rachel. I didn't think — "

"You didn't think?" I snarled, rubbing my temples. "I thought you were such a genius at thinking. But all you seem to be doing is enjoying the neat time you're having. This isn't the Hardy Boys, okay?"

He stood up and walked away. I thought he was going to leave for good this time, but he didn't. He marched around the room, came back and stood in front of me. I stared out the window. His voice was soft and low. "I'm really, really sorry, Red. My dad says I run off in ten different directions and still don't end up where I intended to go."

I had to smother a smile. His dad was right.

"I guess I got a little carried away, too," I muttered. "Sorry if I seem to be blowing hot and cold over this. But this isn't — "

"Yeah, you're right," he said. "It isn't. And I'll try not to . . . you know . . . act like a jerk all the time. You feeling all right?"

I nodded. "I'm okay. I guess we can still watch for it tonight."

He let out a long breath. "Good."

"We'll have to be really quiet," I said. "I wouldn't know how to explain — you know — if you were caught up here."

"Don't worry. Discretion is my middle name. We should be able to sort things out — "

"Logically?"

We looked at each other and I felt lifted by his warm smile. The headache eased a little. Neither of us noticed the next book slide across the desk. It hit the floor with a loud bang. Apparently, someone else agreed, too.

Chapter 15

After he left, I felt both better and worse. Even though he'd tried really hard to tone down his enthusiasm and take things seriously, one half of me couldn't help wondering if, in fact, he was still playing at ghost hunter, while I knew it was real — real and scary and maybe even deadly. That half of me drifted into a restless gloom. "But wait a minute," the other half of me whispered, "at least you have a friend — a friend who wants to help." I took two more aspirins and thought about Will. I closed my eyes and thought about him some more. Then I nodded to myself. It was worth a try. Besides which, I'd already promised.

Overloaded with plans and thoughts and worries, I sagged deeper into my pillows. My throat was really starting to ache again and my head felt stuffed full of damp cardboard bits. As the light faded in the room, I dropped into a fretful sleep.

By eight o'clock in the evening, I was sitting up in bed with a tray on my lap, pushing stringy boiled chicken through a pile of watery carrots. Midnight seemed like days, not hours, away and I wasn't feeling much better.

Ignoring the blackened baked apple that Gladys had squelched onto a pool of lumpy custard, I picked up one of the movie magazines Mitzi had loaned me and settled down to leaf through it. I kept my ears cocked and one eye on the ready for any strange sounds or movements in the room.

Four more hours. Maybe I should have told Will how sick I really was. My head felt as soggy and squashed as that sagging apple on my tray.

"Are you finished, little one?" called Luther from the bottom of the stairs. Before I could answer, the sounds of tinkling glass came up the stairway.

"I'm done," I called back, but the words twisted in my throat and I had a coughing fit. I eyed the tray he was carrying. "I don't think I need any more medicine. I've had lots of sleep. I'm just coughing a bit, that's all." The last thing I needed now was to get drowsy.

"Well, let's see," he said. "How about some of my Very Special Flu Syrup?"

"Didn't I have that last night?"

"No. That was for ordinary cough and flu.

This is for special . . . very special cough and flu." He grinned.

"It won't make me sleepy, will it? I don't want to sleep yet. And I feel fine, honest." I smothered a small cough.

"It will ease your affliction. Give you strength to fight off . . . well . . . those germs, eh?"

Before I could argue, he held a loaded spoon to my lips and I swallowed convulsively.

"Yech! I liked that other one better."

"This one is stronger. It will do you a lot of good, believe me," he said, stepping back. "Necessary good."

I didn't like the way he said that, nodding and winking at the same time. Aunt Irene appeared at the top of the stairs and walked towards the bed, hands clasped in front of her. Mitzi followed close behind, her eyes curious and overbright.

I tried to sit up and demand that they tell me what was happening, but my muscles weren't working. Without warning, my whole body dipped and swayed, leaving my head floating somewhere behind me on its own. Was it the bed swaying, I wondered, as I held tight to the edge of the mattress? No, it was definitely the room that was moving — the walls rippled in waves as if they were being reflected back to me in a fun-house mirror.

Luther, Mitzi and Aunt Irene were sliding back and forth, bigger and smaller. I wanted to reach out and steady everyone, but I couldn't remember where my hands were. Aunt Irene was saying something. Her sharp anxious face moved back and forth, yet came nearer and nearer. Mitzi's hovered beside it, like a pink ball of candyfloss. I giggled. Just like at the circus. Fun houses, and candy-floss curls.

"Rachel, can you . . . hear me?" Aunt Irene asked in a voice that sometimes shouted, sometimes whispered. "Luther! Did . . . give . . . too much?" It was as if someone was fiddling with her dials, turning her volume up and down, louder and softer.

"Better . . . way," Mitzi said, patting Aunt Irene's shoulder in slow motion. "Must . . . sleep . . . communicate . . . healthy body . . . know that."

"You've poisoned me," I tried to shout, but my mouth wouldn't work. These awful people had actually . . . whoops . . . I slid sideways and down, my mind crying, Why? Why?

In the distant mist, I could hear their voices. Why didn't they speak slower and clearer? What were they saying? Was I going to die? Another voice joined theirs, a soothing, sweet voice, saying rest, rest, sleep sleep.

Luther's grinning skull face appeared above the others, looking gentle around the eyes. "Sleep . . . good . . . little one . . . know . . . Irenie . . . fine in the . . . when wakes up . . . clear channel . . . now." He reached over and patted someone's hand. Was it mine?

I wanted desperately to move my arms, to grab at something that would keep me from the dark gluey blackness that was sucking at me. I tried to concentrate on my plans with . . . what was his name? Will. That was it. I had to stay awake, stay alert, keep my eyes wide open. I couldn't let what's-his-name down. The three faces above me backed away until they were pinpoints of pale light and the warm sticky darkness finally closed over me.

Chapter 16

A series of soft thumping sounds hitting the window beside my head woke me up the next morning. Stretching and yawning, I watched a slushy lump of snow drain down the outside pane.

I sat up slowly, expecting to feel horrible. To my surprise, I felt good. Better than that, I felt great. My throat had lost its scratchiness and my head felt clear. I smiled when I remembered the night before. I should have known better than to think that Luther had been trying to kill me.

Leaning over, I peered down at the snowy ground below and saw Will dressed in a plaid jacket and a red ski hat. He was bending over scooping up another snowball. Yanking open the window, I rested my arms on the damp sill and called down, "Hey! I'm awake. What do you want?"

Will straightened up, dropped the snow, put both mittened hands on hips and glared at me. "What do I want? *What* do I *want*? Where the heck were you last night?" He was trying to yell and keep his voice down at the same time. "I stood outside in below zero weather, ankle deep in falling snow and nobody opened up her door like she was supposed to."

"Wait there," I called. "I'll be right down."

When I walked around the corner ten minutes later, Will looked so tall and familiar and solid. Like I'd known him all my life. Here was someone who'd actually waited out in the snow at midnight for me. Suddenly I wanted to hug him. He took a step forward, but stepped back again and frowned. I punched his arm when I saw how flushed his ears had become.

"I was worried about you, you know. You could have at least called," he said. "But you don't look as if you suffered much. Sleep well? For myself, I suffered chilblains and a frozen little toe."

He was trying to sound angry, but he laughed and ducked when I threw the snowball I'd been hiding behind my back.

"Let's walk," I said. "No one's up yet. You'll never guess what? The Fossils drugged me last night!"

"They did? You're kidding! You wanna let me in on why you sound so happy about that little fact?" he exclaimed. "Are you sure they haven't put you on uppers?"

"I didn't say I was happy about it," I protested, leading the way through the front gate.

"But you know, I feel so great, I don't really care. I think the stuff they gave me did it. It made me awfully dizzy at first and I felt like I was dropping down a deep well." I stopped and looked back at the dark brick house. "Luther tricked me. That's the only part I don't like. He said it was just cough syrup. But it wasn't."

"And what happened when you fell down this well?" He sounded worried.

I thought a minute. "Nothing. I woke up when you started using my window for target practice."

"And you feel all right?"

"I feel fabulous! I feel . . ." I threw my arms in the air. "I feel so clean . . . and . . . and new . . . and. . . ."

"And squeaky? You sound like a soap commercial. Follow me, Suds. We've got things to talk about."

He took my arm and steered me down the street to a dingy coffee shop on the corner. I hadn't noticed it before, probably because it was in the opposite direction from school. Inside were six empty booths, the smell of fresh coffee and a row of dirty windows stuffed with gigantic dusty plants that blocked off most of the light from the street.

Over gooey cinnamon buns dripping in butter and mugs of thick hot chocolate, we tried to decide what to do next.

"Did you watch my room from your place last night?" I asked.

He nodded. "And you're going to ask me if I saw something, right?"

"Yes."

"Well, I didn't. Your room was as black as pitch. So at midnight I cased the place and waited at the back door, freezing my backside off, I might add. The house was silent as a tomb."

"Maybe the ghost realized I was dead to the world — his and ours. And he didn't bother coming around. I wish there was some way of talking to him — getting in touch with him. Sounds dumb, eh?"

"Not really. Have you ever tried a ouija board?" he asked around a mouthful of sticky bun.

"No, but I know how they work. There's an alphabet on them, and you use a little pointy board on legs that spells out the words somehow. The spirits are supposed to send messages. Right?"

He nodded and licked his fingers. "Yeah, that's it more or less. There's also a yes and a no on the board, so you can use yes and no type questions. Anyway, I've got one. I got it years ago for Christmas from some crazy uncle."

"Fascinating. So?"

"So I figure we should take the board, go to your room — to do homework we'll say — and set up on that haunted desk of yours. See what happens. And tonight, don't drink or eat a thing they give you. We'll try ghost watching if the ouija doesn't tell us anything."

"I don't think they'll give me any more of that stuff. They only used it to make me feel better.

I'm okay now. Really. I feel great. You wouldn't believe it. I feel so . . ."

Will stood up. "I know, I know — squeaky clean and new. Let's go pick up the ouija board before you drift away in a soap bubble."

Laughing and shoving each other, we headed for the door. I didn't see the other customer in the café right away. I felt his presence first. I turned my head slightly. Out of the corner of my eye, I could just make out someone seated at a table in the darkest corner of the room. Pale blond hair gleamed and a pair of almond-shaped eyes blinked slowly at us from behind an open newspaper. I turned and stared. Roger.

The place had been empty when we'd arrived. I was sure of that. And I'd sat facing the door all the time. No one had come in. How had Roger entered? The back way? He smiled his curly-lipped smile and lifted one finger away from the newspaper in a silent salute. I gave a limp wave back and hustled Will through the door.

"Do you know that guy?" he asked when we were outside. "I've seen him around. There's something creepy about him."

"Funny you should say that," I said, walking quickly away from the café. I shivered in the warm jacket. "That was Roger. Bridgette's true love. I told you about him."

"Hey, was he at that table when we got there?" Will asked, catching up to me. " 'Cause no one came in later. I'd bet on it."

I shrugged. I was busy debating whether to

tell him what else I'd seen in the café. Something just as unnerving as Roger. Back in the dusty corner, behind Roger, a shadow had slid across the wall and back again. And it wasn't Roger's. He'd been sitting quite still while the murky shape skimmed back and forth behind his head. I shivered again.

This was silly. That shadow could have belonged to the waitress working in the kitchen. Wishful thinking. The shadow had wings, like a small bird. There had been no door or window in that corner. At least not that I could make out. Still, I told myself, we had left quickly. Maybe I was wrong. Maybe there'd been a bird feeder outside. Maybe Will noticed if there was a window.

"So that's the guy that takes Bridgette out," Will continued. "I have a feeling that we'd better steer clear of him."

I took the plunge. "Listen, did you see a window in the corner where he was sitting?"

He shook his head. "There's no window. I've sat in that corner."

That shook me silent until we reached Will's house.

"My dad's car's gone. I guess he gave up on me," said Will. "My mom goes to her painting studio on weekends and my dad's supposed to hang around with me. He usually tries to convince me to be his camera bearer while he stalks historic houses. Definitely boring. I think he's out in Plum Coulee or somewhere taking pictures of crumbling farmhouses this morning. Come on in."

I liked his house right off. For one thing, it smelled nice, like clean laundry off the line. And furniture polish. And home cooking that wasn't burned. The furniture was a funny mix of modern and old together, with old-fashioned tables and shiny sideboards next to fat tweedy chairs and woven rugs. Huge plants hung in every room. No dust. No musty smells. Nice. Will led the way up a set of polished stairs and down a hall lined with black and white photos of old houses and farm buildings.

I followed him into a big room that looked like a science lab. There were shelves and low built-in cupboards covered with all kinds of chemistry and science equipment and quite a few glassed-in boxes filled with displays of beetles, butterflies and Indian arrowheads. On a wide desk stood a full computer set-up with filing cabinets and stacks of cardboard boxes underneath.

In one corner was a long, narrow, unmade bed. Clothes were piled on it, and on the floor, and on every surface that wasn't loaded down with books and miscellaneous junk. Near the window stood a jumbo recliner chair. A table beside it was crowded with empty cola bottles and half-eaten bags of chips and cheezies. It was altogether a great room.

"Welcome to my abode," he said, off-handedly. "Now, where did I put it? I dug it out last night. Took it with me," he glared at me, "into the freezing night, and brought it back unused. Aah! Here it is. Le Ouija. And the little table is called the planchette. I looked that up."

He held up a ouija board in one hand and a

125

tiny heart-shaped table in the other. I had some very big doubts about a toy bringing in the young man in the brown dressing gown.

"Will, it's just like yesterday. This is all a game to you. Like this dumb plastic toy in your hand. Do you really think that a real ghost is going to talk to us on that?"

He looked hurt. "It is an accepted way of communicating with the other side. I read that in a book. Besides, anything's worth a try, right? I think it's worth a try."

"But, Will, it's a plastic toy."

"Let's keep an open mind, shall we?" Will sniffed. "For someone who wants to solve the mystery of the ghost in your attic, I think you're being awfully closed-minded about this."

"All right. Bring the stupid thing. But it won't work."

He hid the board in a pile of school notebooks and stuck the little planchette in his jacket pocket. "You know," he said, "I'm amazed. All these things happen to someone like you. You really don't have a very open mind, do you?"

"I have an open mind! How else could all those shadows and sounds get in there?" I said. "Maybe my mind is too open!"

"What?"

"Nothing . . . never mind. Let's go try to raise a ghost on a stupid, silly, heart-shaped plastic table."

Chapter 17

We were still arguing away when we pushed open the back door of 135 Cambric and found ourselves surrounded by the Fossils. "Where have you been?" demanded Aunt Irene, grabbing me by the shoulders and examining me from head to toe. "You weren't supposed to go out today. You had us worried sick."

"I was — "

"Just worried sick," repeated Gladys, patting my yellow tam and blinking rapidly behind her thick glasses.

"Now, now, I told you she'd be fine," said Mr. Basely.

"So did I," said Luther proudly. "And just look at her! Perfect! I told you I'd fix her up, didn't I?"

"I'd have known if she wasn't all right," said Mitzi, "but still, one can't be too careful. Who's this with you, Rachel? Will, isn't it? Out playing in the lovely wet snow, I'll wager, eh?" She was eating a thick wedge of toast smeared with marmalade. "No harm done, kids, right? She's fine, Irenie. Don't fuss, for Pete's sakes."

Aunt Irene bristled. "And why shouldn't I worry? I care what happens to her."

"And we don't, I suppose?" Mitzi asked, her cheeks turning brick red. Her pink hair wobbled indignantly. "It's more than just a job to us, too. Just because she's your blood kin doesn't mean . . ."

"Mitzi's quite right, Irene. That's the third or fourth time you've accused us of not caring," said Mr. Basely, eyebrows stiffening. "Why just the other day — "

"You just finished saying you weren't worried," Aunt Irene said between her teeth. "You just finished saying that."

"What I said, Irene," Mr. Basely replied, adjusting his tweed jacket and holding himself to his full height, "what I said was that I wasn't worried about her . . . I mean to say, that I knew she was fine."

"You see, everyone? He just admitted — "

"Wait!" I shouted.

"Rachel!" said Aunt Irene. "Please dear, don't bellow. And don't interrupt your elders."

"But I just wanted to say I was sorry. I didn't know I had to tell you where I was going. I never had to tell Dad. And when Joanna was around, she couldn't have cared less . . . so . . . I'm sorry. I can see you were worried, Aunt Irene." No one was more surprised than I was at what had just come out of my mouth. What can I tell you?

"Now, isn't that nice?" chirped Gladys.

"Yes, it is," said Mr. Basely, smiling down at me.

"Good kid," said Mitzi, thumping me on the back. "So, are you two here for a bite to eat?"

"We've got homework," said Will.

"Yeah," I added, "I missed yesterday and I was already behind, being new and all. Will's going to help me catch up on some of the math. We'll work up in my room."

"Well now, I don't know about that," said Aunt Irene. "The two of you up there alone?"

"Don't be silly, Irene," said Mitzi. "Go on, you kids. Want anything to eat first? Toast?" She held up her own.

"No thanks, we'll just get to work," I said, pushing Will towards the hall door. I had a hunch Aunt Irene wasn't finished and I wasn't wrong.

"Mitzi, I'll thank you very much not to play down my concerns or for that matter my authority over my niece," she snipped. "After all, she is my niece. And I don't want . . ."

All the Fossils started in then. Will and I backed out of the room. The swinging door cut them off to a low rumble. We ran up the stairs like mad, and when we got to the attic, fell into the stuffed chairs, breathless and laughing.

"Boy, your dad can't say you're not being looked after, can he?" Will said, wiping his eyes. "They'll be putting a leash on you next."

At the mention of Dad, I stopped laughing. Dad. I felt something deep inside me crack and splinter into sharp little pieces. Maybe it came from knowing that Aunt Irene and the Fossils were worried when my own parents didn't seem to care two pins.

I felt myself swamped by a wave of unhappiness so powerful that my senses pulled back, withdrew, until everything outside me was blocked off. Will's laughter became faint echoing sounds down a distant corridor.

Another voice stirred inside my mind and tried to say something — a new voice, gentle and deep and urgent. Where had I heard it before? I sat up. Dad? No. It was the same voice I'd heard the night before when Luther had given me the medicine. I listened hard, but couldn't make out what it was saying. Hesitatingly at first, then with more confidence, I allowed my thoughts to reach out to it. *Rachel*. With the sound of my name, I felt things, things I hadn't felt for a long time — understanding — warmth — a strange wonderful sense of growing outside myself, and of touching something deep inside me at the same time. There! It said my name again. Listen, it said, I must tell you . . . you must listen. I leaned into the gentle sounds, but abruptly they stopped, followed by a penetrating hiss and something else — the swishing of dark wings.

"No!" I cried, covering my ears.

I felt a warm hand on my arm. Will's face peered into mine.

"Hey," I heard him say, "what's up? You okay? You look funny, all of a sudden. Did you see something?"

With the touch of Will's hand, everything, except a soft humming around my head, stopped.

"What's happening, Rachel?"

"There's something . . ." I said, my voice a harsh whisper. "Someone . . . something is here with us. There. Did you hear it, Will? A sweet, sweet voice. Did you hear it?"

He looked around. "No. Where?"

"From everywhere," I said, sweeping my arm lazily through the air. "Put the ouija on the desk. On the top of the desk."

Will hesitated, listening. "No. Look. I don't think we should do this. Okay? Your eyes look odd . . . sort of glassy."

"We have to do it," I said, slowly and carefully. "Will, we have to."

He nodded, looking scared. I watched him set the ouija up. As soon as our fingers touched the little plastic planchette, it trembled and moved.

"Hey! Wow!" exclaimed Will. "Feel that?"

"Shhh. Quiet."

The little plastic heart stopped trembling.

"Jeez, look at that," Will said, "it stopped."

"Please, Will," I whispered, "please don't talk."

Pale and uncertain he leaned forward as if to say something, then pressed his lips together and nodded. We waited, fingers resting lightly on the planchette. Slowly it came to life again under our fingertips.

"Who . . . who are you?" I asked the ouija softly.

"It's moving! Are you pushing it?" Will breathed.

"No!" I said sharply. "And don't speak. Please!"

"Well, something's moving it and it isn't me," he said, ignoring my warning. "Lookit it! It's going to the J . . . to the O . . . to the H . . . is that last one an N?" The point of the heart swerved over to the painted YES on the board. "Yes, it said yes! Is your name John?"

Again the planchette swerved to the YES. I held my breath.

"John what?" asked Will. "Look at it go! What's it spelling? RACHEL. Rachel. His last name is Rachel?"

The planchette moved so fast that it left our fingers in the air above the board. No, it said. No. No. No. It flew back and forth, as if shaking its head, always returning to the NO. I shoved Will's hand off the little heart.

"Hey! Now we'll lose contact for good, Rach!" he cried.

"Don't. Let me. He wants to talk to me."

"Yes. Yes. Yes." The planchette raced across the board. "B . . . E . . . W . . . A . . . R . . . E."

"Beware?" My voice caught in my throat. "What . . . what should I beware of?"

"Maybe we should stop," whispered Will.

"Wait. It's moving again."

The planchette searched for the letters, slowly this time, almost as if its energy was wearing out. "T . . . H . . . E . . . O . . . T . . . H . . . E . . . R . . . O . . . N . . . E."

"What does that mean?" Will asked. "I can't make it out. Is it some kind of command?"

"No. No. No," scratched the planchette.

"I see!" I cried. "He's saying The Other One. Beware of The Other One. Right, John?"

"Yes, yes," it said.

"But . . . who is that? Do you mean someone downstairs? Aunt Irene or one of the other people? Or do you mean that shadow that's following me?"

"No. No. Yes." The planchette flew across the board.

"He's confused," said Will. "So am I. You're asking too many questions."

"John, I'm sorry," I said. "Maybe you could pause between each word. Do you hear me?"

The little heart waited and then scraped its way to the YES. Then it began to pick up speed again. This time, though, it waited a second or two between words. "Yes, he is near you. He watches and feels your anger," it spelled. "He is attracted by it. He needs it. Warn them. Tell them the stone is here." I spoke slowly to him. "Who? Warn who? What stone? Can't you make it clearer?"

The ouija moved, slowly scraping the board in circles, then it stopped.

"See? You shouldn't have pushed my hand off," said Will. "Jeez, Rachel, no wonder it's confused. You asked too many questions again. You've overloaded its circuits."

"That's not why!" I said furiously. "He's . . . John's getting tired. I can feel it."

But Will wasn't looking at me. He was staring pop-eyed at something else. "Do you see it?" he croaked. "Do you see it?"

"Yes," I whispered.

A hand outlined in delicate blue lights and little electric flashes lowered its long fingers onto the planchette beside mine. As soon as they touched, my fingers felt glued to the board. At the same time, I felt the now familiar warm electric current — the same sensation I'd had when Aunt Irene and Luther had touched my hand — move up my arm. Then it moved back down and through my fingers. Slowly the little table moved. Will spoke its message.

"He-wants-what-I-have-you-must-be-prepared-Rachel-my-dear-your-anger-it-is-not-good-I-am-so-very-tired-you-must-warn-them-about-stone-stay-close." The planchette slowed even more. "Tired-energy-gone-waited-too-long-he-would-know-then-and-use-you-too-long-cannot . . . wait . . . do nothing . . . I . . . will . . . come . . . again," the little heart inched through the last word, ". . . tonight."

The hand was fading.

"But, don't go yet. Who are you talking about? Who is that shadow?" My throat closed and I choked off a sob. "What should I do?"

The hand lifted, placed its faint cool light over mine and was gone.

Chapter 18

"I'm telling you for the last time, no!" I said fiercely.

We'd spent the last half hour arguing. Will had demanded to know about the shadow I'd kept referring to and I'd finally broken down and told him and I'd followed up with the Warnings. Now I regretted it.

For the first time, I think he was really truly scared.

"This is not funny any more Rachel," he said angrily. "We don't know what we're playing around with. I'd heard that ouijas could be dangerous, because gullible kids get carried away and scare themselves silly, but . . . that hand!" He pulled his hair until it stood straight up. "How do we know who that was? Maybe he's not a good ghost." He leaned into my face. "We have to talk to an adult about this."

"I'm not talking to my aunt or the rest of them until I've had a chance to talk to him again. To John. He's trying to warn me. I know it. You know it. About someone or something. This shadow, probably. How do I know it isn't connected to them downstairs?"

"All right, all right! But honestly, Rachel, the way you've described these shadows — shadows I might add, that keep following you around — well, it really gives me the total creeps. Why didn't you tell me sooner? And about these 'warning' things."

"Get real, Will. You'd have thought I was nuts."

He shook his head. "I'll tell you what's nuts! This is nuts! Rachel. That hand was real. Get it? *Real*! We both saw it. I think we're mucking around in something that could be dangerous."

"Now you tell me? You thought this was all so neat, remember? What did you call it? Intriguing," I countered. "You don't have to be involved with it any more. Or with me. You can go home right now. Go ahead. Leave." I was yelling at him, but in the back of my mind I knew that if he left, I probably couldn't go on alone. That surprised me. Some tough country kid.

He ran true to form, thank goodness. "That's your answer to me every time," he shouted. "Right! Leave! I'll just leave you here alone to face it all! First you tell me I'm trivial and now when I get worried and realize how serious this whole mess is, you tell me, just like that, that I can go." He threw his hands in the air. "I'll tell

136

you this, Rachel MacCaw, you're not pushing me out of this. Take my word for it."

"Are you really sure?" I asked, my voice high and quivery.

He stared at me. "Do you want me to write it in blood?" He looked over his shoulder and shivered dramatically. "Forget I said that. Just as soon as my folks and your Fossils are asleep, I'm over here, okay? If you're so determined to be Nancy Drew, I'd better be George."

"George was a girl," I said, smiling shakily.

"Whatever," he continued. "But I'll be here. Got it?"

I nodded. "Okay. Here. Take my back-door keys. They should all be asleep by midnight downstairs. Come then."

"Right. Now I won't have to stand outside wondering if you've been done in or something."

"Nice thought. Good thing I'm not worried about them," I sneered, but inside I wasn't sneering. Inside I was pretty wobbly.

"Come on," he said, "let's go to my place. We need a break."

I followed him down to the next floor and thought I heard a door quietly close down the hall. Had one of the Fossils been listening? We'd been making enough noise. The hall was empty and quiet. We continued to the main floor. We'd just reached the bottom step when I heard Aunt Irene's voice. She was standing by a small hall table talking on the phone, her back towards us.

"Yes, yes, Alan. She's fine. I told you. Yes, doing well at school . . . I imagine. No. No problems. Don't worry. It's just a mild cold. I keep telling you everything is just fine. Are you? I hope so." She looked over her shoulder. "Well . . . yes . . . goodbye for now."

"No!" I ran and grabbed the receiver. "Don't hang up! Dad! Dad?" It was too late. Only a dial tone answered back. "Why didn't you call me?" I yelled at her. "That was Dad, wasn't it? I need to talk to him! Why did you hang up? You saw me standing right here."

Aunt Irene straightened her shoulders and said in a stiff tone, "I'm awfully sorry, Rachel. I can't imagine what I was thinking of. But your father only had a few moments. He was at a weigh station. He says to tell you he's fine. He said goodbye so quickly, I couldn't stop him. I'm sorry." She wouldn't look me in the eye. She smoothed her cardigan sweater and cleared her throat.

"You aren't sorry," I shouted. "You did it deliberately. I bet he's called lots of times. You said, 'I *keep telling you* everything's fine.' So, he *has* called before. Why don't you let me talk to him?" I slammed down the receiver and stalked down the hall to the front door.

I was shaking so hard I was sure that the floor under my feet was cracking open. A keening wind whistled deep in my ears. Across my line of vision came the familiar and terrible flap of wings. I stopped. John had said my anger attracted The Other One. Was this it? Who was that laughing? I put my hands to my ears. Why was everything so loud?

"Rachel."

Who was that? The voice sounded familiar. I felt a tug on my arm and Will's face swam towards me through a murky curtain of fading light. He pushed my jacket through the mist. His voice came down a narrow tunnel. "Take this. Put it on. We'll go out for a while. All right?"

I stared at him. Then nodded slowly. The thick gauze over my eyes was thinning. The wind was slowing down and I could barely hear the swish, swish of retreating wings.

"Rachel? My dear?"

I glared at Aunt Irene. She moved her hand as if to touch me, but drew it back and smoothed her sweater once again. She turned and walked away, that same hand reaching out to steady herself against the wall.

Will helped me on with my boots, opened the door and pulled me outside. A fat orange sun was sitting on top of the house across the street. Dark inky-blue shadows stretched across the snow-rutted road.

"I told her to go away. And she did. I did that once before and she went. She always looks so sad when I do that, but she deserved it this time, didn't she? I told *her*, didn't I?" I babbled.

"You didn't say a word after you almost destroyed the phone," Will answered. "You stood there like your brain had locked in neutral. You did that upstairs, too."

What was he saying? I was sure I'd told Aunt Irene to get lost. "You mean she left without my speaking?"

"Yeah. She just turned and walked away."

"I told her to go away," I insisted. "If I didn't

say it out loud, do you think she read my mind? After that, those awful wings showed up and started thrashing around."

"They did? I didn't hear or see anything. Do you think it's John doing it? Or this other one he talked about?" He looked altogether uncertain. "And as far as her reading your mind, I'd believe just about anything now," he muttered.

"I don't know anything any more," I said, "except you'd probably be better off taking pictures of old farms with your dad rather than hanging around with me."

Heavy flakes of snow, like goosefeathers out of a giant pillowcase, started to drift down. I stopped and stared at one that dangled like a fuzzy ornament from the thin branch of a small tree. Will walked up behind me and put his hand on my shoulder. I leaned my back against his chest for just the breath of a second.

"Will? Am I going crazy, do you think?"

He put both hands on my shoulders and turned me to face him. "Then we're both going nuts, Red. You keep forgetting — I saw John in the window even before you came and I saw the hand today. You are seeing and hearing exactly what you think you're hearing and seeing. As far as I'm concerned, your Fossils know more than they're saying, all right. I could see it in your aunt's face."

He gave me a gentle push towards his house. "And don't look now, but the whole crew is peering out the front window at us."

I glanced over my shoulder in time to see the lace curtain twitch across the glass of the parlour window. Will pushed me again and when I didn't move, he took my hand and pulled me across the street.

"Hey, never mind. I think they're worried about you, that's all. I really do. Maybe we'll know more tonight. Look, there's my dad's car. He's home. We'll see what he has to say."

His dad? "Will! No! He'd really think we were nuts. Or making it up."

"He's a neat guy, honest — "

I held onto his sleeve. "Will. No. I mean it. If we do see him, let's just casually ask him about the house. Please?"

He shrugged. "Okay." He led me through the glassed-in porch and down a long hallway into a bright kitchen with ferny plants in the windows.

"So, do you think your aunt is telling your dad a bunch of B.S. whenever he calls?" he asked, as he rummaged around in the refrigerator. "And if she is, why? Those old people must be involved with John somehow."

"It sounds like it, doesn't it?" I said.

"But why would she tell him a bunch of lies? She'd have to have a reason."

I shook my head. The last few rays of sunlight slanted through the kitchen window and lit up his spiky hair from behind. It warmed a big bowl of apples on the counter and their sweet breath filled the room. Everything in this house seemed so snug and . . . well, contented.

"You with me here, Red?" Will asked, his voice concerned.

I smiled. "Yeah. I was just thinking how much

I liked your house. Joanna, my mom, well, she just didn't have the knack." I took off my jacket and threw it over a chair. "I just wish Aunt Irene had let me speak to Dad."

"At least you know he was calling to check up. That's something, isn't it?"

I nodded. "Yeah. That's something."

"Peanut butter okay? You get the bread. In that old apple box over there that my mother decided was just perfect for her crunchy rustic home-made bread. Don't worry," he said laughing, when he saw me checking the loaf, "no zucchini bits. So, the way I figure it, all our answers lie in John's electric hands. Hope he tells us what stake he's got in this." He slapped half a jar of peanut butter on four slices of bread. "Now, if a ghost is the main character . . ."

"Hello, what have we here?" said a deep voice from the kitchen door. "Did I hear you say something about ghosts?"

"Oh, hi, Pop. This's Rachel. She lives across the street. At 135. With Miss MacCaw and the others. Moved in a couple of weeks ago. We were just . . . uh . . . just going to track you down and ask you something. But first we needed some food. We're working on a school project together."

"A project for school? On ghosts?" asked Mr. Lennox. "Sounds positively fascinating."

Mr. Lennox wasn't at all like I'd pictured him. He was short for one thing. With a chubby face, big soft brown eyes and a small nose. And almost no hair. But when he smiled, I could see Will's lopsided grin in there somewhere. He was wearing dark green cords and a big yellow sweater.

"No," said Will through a mouthful. "On old houses, not a ghost. Although we were hoping we could work one in. We've got to write a play for English. But it has to be based on local history. Right, Rachel?"

Mr. Lennox smiled and said, "So, Rachel, what do you and Will want to know?"

"Well . . . uh . . . we . . . uh . . ."

"We wanna know what you know about 135. Rachel's place. You know lots about the old houses on Cambric, right? So what about 135?"

"Now, that place is a curiosity all right," Mr. Lennox said, slowly, nodding his head. "It's one of the few houses original to this area. What's really amazing is that it's only had three owners in all those years."

"Who owned it first?" asked Will.

"A man named Leach. A doctor." He took one of Will's peanut butter messes and bit into it. "I don't think there's too much to know about him. He was sort of a recluse in old age."

"What else?" Will asked.

"Ah, you and Rachel wouldn't be all that interested in local gossip," Mr. Lennox said.

"No, really Pop, we would, wouldn't we, Rach?" Will said.

"Okay," Mr. Lennox said, leaning against the counter and taking two more big bites. "Well, it's curious . . . I talked to a few old people in the neighbourhood and believe it or not a couple of their parents knew him. At least as far as anyone knew him." It was all a bit muffled by

143

the peanut butter, but I think that's what he said. "Every one of them described him as an eccentric, and oddball."

"How?" Will and I said simultaneously. I held my breath.

He took another peanutty bite and grimaced. "All they said was that he was into mysterious doings — like black magic but *not* black magic. I couldn't pin any of them down. I do know that he had private patients who stayed in the house. The records say that he was just an ordinary GP who ran a small hospice for TB patients. Apparently he was a leading authority on the disease. Consumption, as it was called, was not uncommon back then."

Will handed him a glass of chocolate milk. Mr. Lennox eyed it suspiciously, then shrugged and took a few gulps. He smacked his lips and continued. "You have to remember that medicine was still pretty primitive. Most people were terrified of consumption. A lot of superstition around it."

"Say, Pop, this Leach guy, did he live at 135 very long? Like, what else do you know about the house?" Will shoved a big pack of Oreos across the table. His dad took a handful.

Mr. Lennox pursed his lips thoughtfully. "Let me see. He had the house built around 1870. He lived there until the thirties or forties. Lived to a ripe old age. Then it was sold to a couple who ran it as a boarding-house until only a few years ago. These old people of Rachel's bought it last year sometime."

I expected him to ask about the Fossils and

why I was living with them, but he didn't. I liked him for that.

"In fact," he continued, "we looked at buying it ourselves. A great place. But too big for us. And it needed a great deal of work. So we moved in here."

"His . . . his name wasn't *John* Leach by any chance, was it?" I asked.

"No. No, it was Edward, I think. Yes. Edward Leach," Mr. Lennox said.

"Did he have a son John?" Will asked.

He shook his head. "No wife. No kids." Mr. Lennox lowered his voice. "Do we have a ghostly presence on the premises? Is that why you were talking ghosts?" He made an Oooo sound. Very ghostlike, he thought, I'm sure.

"We just figured it might make a good story, that's all," said Will, shrugging. "But we're supposed to base our play on fact, so it was just a . . . a stupid idea."

"I see, I see, I see. Well, too bad," offered Mr. Lennox. "Ghosts are always fun. The other kids would have liked it, I'm sure."

"Yeah," Will said. "So, what do you think of all this stuff, Dad? Ghosts and things."

"Ghosts?"

"Yeah, ghosts. Do you believe in them? Just as an acadamic question, of course."

Mr. Lennox looked surprised. "Me? I don't know, Will. I'm a sceptic, I guess. I prefer to believe in what I can see. I have my doubts. But on the other hand, I like to think I have an open mind."

His mind wasn't open enough for what we

145

saw. And I could tell from Will's frown that he was thinking the same thing.

He shrugged. "Oh well, back to the drawing board, Rachel."

"We were only kidding around anyway. We've got to get serious about this, Will, or we'll never finish the project." I took my jacket off the back of the chair. "I've gotta go. We can work on it tomorrow."

Just then a tall woman swept into the room, scarves and sandy-coloured pony-tail flying out behind. She dumped a pile of books and a metal tool case on the table. "I'm just too tired to paint today," she said. "So I've come home to bake that new apple bread recipe I found. Oh! Hello! I didn't see this young person when I stormed in." She smiled at me with an intense concentration. "Will? Introduce us."

"Oh. Yeah. This is Rachel, Mom. She lives with Miss MacCaw and the others across the street. We're working on a school project for English. We're — "

"You live with all those old people across the street? How did that happen?" she asked, her look intensifying.

I had a feeling that Will and his dad didn't get to finish many sentences. Her paint-stained fingers reminded me of Joanna. That was all I needed. Only this one was more like a couple of Joanna's friends from the city. They led women's encounter groups, cooked with tofu (don't even bother, it's inedible gunk), and thought they knew what made you tick without even knowing you.

"I've gotta go," I said pulling my jacket on. "Thanks, Mr. Lennox. I'll see you tomorrow, Will."

"Don't rush off, dear," said Mrs. Lennox, her concerned face looking me up and down. "Why not stay for dinner? You look like you could do with a decent meal. I'm sure those old people eat nothing but tea and toast. I've been in there a few times to check up on them, but they seem to be quite vocal in their independence. How on earth did you end up living there? Oh dear, I've scared you off. I hope not. I do have a tendency to mow people down, I'm afraid. I have, haven't I? Scared you off, I mean."

"No! No, honest. I've got to get home. Thanks anyways," I said, backing out of the room.

Will followed me to the front door. "Hey, she won't bite, you know. She just comes on a little strong, that's all. We could talk to her."

"Oh, sure. Let's tell her we saw a ghost named John up in my attic room. And then she'd be over in a flash poking her nose in where it's not wanted," I snapped. "I can tell a do-gooder when I see one. They all have that look in their eye. One of my teachers had it. And after Joanna left, he stuck us with a social worker who had it. I bet your mother is solving little problems around the neighbourhood all the time. Right?"

"Good grief!" Will cried, clutching his chest. "I didn't know! Imagine! I have a mother who cares about people! I should turn her into the cops."

"You know exactly what I mean. She'd be butting in if she heard about our ghost. Probably notify someone to take me away and find therapy for you."

We were standing in the unheated porch and our breath hung around our heads in small clouds of moisture.

Will leaned against the doorjamb. "Yeah, you're right. She gives out zucchini loaves by the dozen. She took in five cats, two dogs, and one foster kid this past summer alone. What can I say? I love her, but she's definitely sick."

We looked at each other and laughed. Reaching out one long arm, Will rested a hand on my shoulder. "You'll be okay? Do you still want to go through with it tonight? I promise I'll lock her up so she won't tag along."

I nodded. "Yeah. I want to. And John did say he'd be back."

He leaned forward and put his free hand on my other shoulder. Looking closely into Will's dark curious eyes, I knew I was changing inside. I wasn't sure I wanted to, but I knew I was. He smiled down at me and I felt a wave of something that made all the little bits and pieces inside fit together again, calm and happy and safe. When his eyes came closer, I saw the fine line of lashes and the shiny dark brows and my heart tightened and felt full at the same time.

"I . . . uh . . . guess I'd better get back," I said softly, after we'd kissed. His lips had felt like warm silk and my hands slid down the smoothness of his back over his plaid shirt.

"Yeah. Okay. See you later," he croaked, then cleared his throat. "You'd better let go first or I'll just stand here all afternoon."

148

I pulled my arms away surprised. I couldn't even remember how they'd got around him. I was just in time, because his mother's head popped around the edge of the door. "Sure you won't change your mind, Rachel?" she asked, showing her teeth in a let's-all-be-friends kind of grin.

"Thanks, but I've got to get home. Thanks anyway," I stammered, and walked out of the house and into the street. Trudging through the snow, I found myself blushing when I thought of what she'd have said if she'd caught us kissing. Probably something really cute. It wasn't until I got right up to the wrought-iron fence around 135 that something jolted me back to the present.

Somebody was creeping along the hedge that ran below the veranda on the south side of the house. I saw a man's shadow flicker between the bare branches. He was keeping his head down, moving quickly.

I slid behind the wide trunk of an oak, my breath held tight in my throat. Dusk had moved in quickly, and the afternoon sun had already rolled off the roof behind the house across the street. Even so, I was able to make out who it was — Bridgette's Roger.

Chapter 19

Roger moved quickly, looking left and right before sliding across open ground to a small group of trees huddled in the corner of the yard. He sprinted over the fence in one smooth movement and disappeared down the street. The dusky light seemed to close around him like a grey cloak.

I waited, thinking hard. If he'd been visiting Bridgette, why was he acting like a commando sniper? I walked down the cleared path around the other side. Turning the corner, I saw something that stopped me dead in my tracks.

Someone was standing at the far corner, peering down the same side of the house that Roger had crept along. It was a small figure covered in layers of black fabric. One of the layers ended in a kind of deep hood.

Strange noises were coming from the small bundle — hollow whistling noises — like wind down a tunnel. The figure swayed and a queer rusty voice cried out, "I'll see you. I will! I will! I'll see you and then I'll know. I'll know you," before dropping to soft angry mutterings. I was about to back around my corner again when the bundle lifted its hands and pushed the hood back. Two bright red barrettes were stuck in the straight hair.

"G-Gladys? Is that you?" I asked.

The bundle of scarves and capes whirled around. It was Gladys, all right. And yet it wasn't Gladys. Her eyes were wide, yet they didn't seem to recognize me at all. Her lips were pulled back in a snarl and her big soft nose was high and sharp in her ragged face.

The black-stockinged legs and white sneakers lifted and stretched in slow motion away from me. Her small crooked hands were raised palm up, as if trying to hold me off.

"Gladys! It's me. Rachel!" I cried.

Gladys looked over her shoulder. "Danger," she croaked. "Look out, child. You shouldn't be here." It didn't sound like Gladys at all.

She ducked, putting her hands over her head. A huge shadow appeared over the prickly hedge and flew silently across the snow towards us. When it reached Gladys, she fell forward as if hit from behind. The shadow hovered above the sprawled figure before spreading over her like thick black oil. Gladys disappeared underneath.

"No!" I cried, running forward. "Get away!"

I slithered through the snow and fell across her. As soon as our bodies touched, the shadow pulled away and disappeared.

"Gladys? Gladys? Are you okay?" I whispered.

"My goodness, that was quite a slippery spot, wasn't it, Rachel dear?" said a muffled voice below. "Give me a hand, there's a love."

I gave her a hand up and she rose shakily to her feet.

"What's happening?" I asked, dusting the snow off her.

"I was out feeding my birds," she said in a quavery voice, "and I'd just returned to the kitchen when that horrible big yellow cat appeared out of nowhere and tried to attack two little sparrows. Well, I ran out. You can imagine!" She looked confused. "And, uh, I . . . let me see . . . I must have chased it off and that's when I fell. And you fell on top of me. That poor cat. Terrible of me, I know. Imagine. Me, of all people, chasing off a cat."

"Did you see Roger?" I asked. "Weren't you watching him? He was running along the side of the house."

Gladys searched for something lost in her mind. "No. Did I? No, I don't think so. When I saw that awful cat I ran out and flapped my arms and made a lot of noise. That usually works. Oh dear . . ." Her voice trailed off. "He must be a stray. Poor thing. And hungry. You can hardly blame him. And yet, I think I was so angry I wanted to kill him." She leaned on me, puffing and blowing.

We walked towards the house, me busy wondering what Roger was doing creeping around, Gladys muttering about the problems of keeping cats and birds living in what she called "shared harmony."

Gladys went to lie down, and I slipped back outside, keeping a sharp eye open for shadows and skinny skulking men. The snow was fresh and new, and I could see my own and Gladys's footprints, and a little farther, the crater Gladys made when she fell. Along the far side of the wall, there was another set of footprints, leading in the direction Roger had taken. The only thing was, the prints weren't big and deep like a man's. No, what I was looking at were the pawprints of a big cat on the run. I followed them to the front fence, to the exact spot that Roger had jumped over. There was not a human print in sight.

Chapter 20

By eleven-thirty that night, I still hadn't worked out how Roger had managed his disappearing footprints acts. Phoning Will right afterwards hadn't helped either.

"Holy cow, Rachel! Maybe he *was* the cat. You know — changed his shape into a cat."

For some reason, I remembered the big marmalade cat on my window sill. I remembered his yellow unblinking stare through the window. Could it be? It was too bizarre to think about.

"That's crazy," I said loudly. "That's absolutely crazy!"

"Rachel." Will's voice came back, all reason and calmness. "I'd believe just about anything now. I'd even believe Roger hovered above the snow — that he glided two inches above it. I'd even believe it if you told me he was a ghost. Maybe he *is* a ghost!"

"Maybe I know now why I shouldn't have called you. You're just plain nuts," I said, wearily.

"Yeah? And nutty isn't seeing a blue hand on a ouija board, I suppose?"

"We both saw that. That's not nutty." I heard the meaningful silence over the telephone line and sighed. "Okay, I see what you mean. But Gladys acted so weird. She told me to step back, 'cause there was danger. And then afterwards, she didn't remember a thing."

"We've already agreed that the Fossils are involved," he said. "Maybe she was pretending to forget. The thing is — well, I don't know how you're going to like this, but it seems to me that you're the centre of all the action. John knows who you are. This shadow seems to be around you and no one else. And now you see Roger, the cat burglar, creeping around outside."

A funny feeling went right through me. I guess I'd known that I was important to some scheme the Fossils were a part of. What a joke. Tossed off by my parents to land in the middle of some ghost production. The only problem was, I hadn't been given my lines yet.

"You still there?" Will asked.

"Yeah. So now what?"

"Okay. Let's go over what you just told me. No footprints except a big cat's. That's what you saw, right? Or didn't see, I guess. So, let's just accept it as part of the whole scare package. And carry on, okay? Agreed?"

There didn't seem to be anything else to do but agree. So there I was at eleven-thirty, stum-

155

bling around in the dark, wishing the only drama in my life was worrying about the frizz in my hair. While other teenagers were watching a Tom Hanks movie or were eating pizza with their friends, I was creeping up and down the halls of a crumbling house, listening at each and every door to make sure the oddball tenants behind them were asleep, so that an oddball boy and me (ditto) could talk to a ghost with a ouija board. Truly insane.

The downstairs was dark and silent, and upstairs seemed the same — at least there weren't any shafts of lamplight sliding under any doors. I sighed with relief when I heard stereo snoring coming from the Dubbles's room. So far so bad. I followed the skinny little beam of light from my pen-light flash back to the attic. Once there, I collapsed into one of the armchairs. Suddenly I was bone-sagging tired. I struggled to keep my eyes open. Will and I had agreed that the lights should stay off. Even so, some light from a street lamp bounced off the snow below, and lit part of the room with a pale eerie glow, sharply outlining some of the arches and turning others into murky caves.

Once, twin shafts of light slid around the walls and I felt my soggy bones jump in my body. Then, just as suddenly, the room fell back into semi-darkness. A car rumbled past on the snow-clogged road below. I let out a snort of laughter. A dumb car. That's all it was. People outside were going about their ordinary everyday lives. Lucky them. My weary eyelids had a mind of their own after that. I was just floating away when — what was that? I sat up, heart pounding.

"Will? Will? That you?" I whispered.

There it was again. I listened hard. It wasn't Will. It was something else. Something — there it was again — something was being dragged across the floor. Behind the store-room door! Why hadn't I looked behind it before I sat down? I eased off the chair, crept forward and pressed my ear to the wood, my hand on the glass knob.

Nothing.

"Whewff! I must have been dreaming," I muttered, turning to creep back to my chair.

But there it was again. *Scrape, swush . . . scrape, swush.* I looked towards the stairs. I'd have to make a run for it and get Will. But wait. Think. Think. What if it was John behind the door? I groped in my pocket for my little flashlight and turned it on. At that moment, the door handle beside me clicked and the door swung open.

A smell, stale and dusty, but mixed with a horrible sweetness flowed out. And with it came the shadow. I could hear the slow heavy swish of huge wings near my head, felt it touch my shoulders, then swirl around me. I tried to move, to run. It held me tight. The thin stab of light from the pen-light cut through the shadow, and in its feeble glow I saw something moving across the floor. Away from me. It was solid. And it was wearing blue jeans. It slid quickly out of the flashlight's gleam. The lid of a trunk crashed down. A man cursed loudly.

"Who-who is it?" I called out. "Can you help me?" I felt the shadow's weight close around me, pressing its sickening sweet-rotten stench into my face, suffocating me.

"NO! Help!" I cried, but my tiny voice drifted and echoed far into the pulsating presence that was pressing, pressing around me. As it tightened, I sensed its power — a concentrated rage, but at the same time an exhilarated glee. Every pore in my body was filling up with the same anger and excitement.

Just as my legs began to crumble under me, a swirling light filled the attic. The shadow's rage grew, until I thought it might explode, then abruptly I felt it pull back, and it simply let me go. I staggered forward, gulping air deep into my lungs. At the same time, I heard someone scuttle towards the back wall of the store-room.

With the help of the light, I could see the jean-clad legs and part of a leather jacket. Funny how at times like that your mind registers little details — like the half-moon-shaped button on the bottom cuff of the jacket. The shadow, once so huge and terrifying, grew smaller and followed quickly, like a phantom bat, its wings slicing through everything that stood in its way.

"Will?" I said, turning to the light. "Did you see who that was?"

But it wasn't Will, this swirling cone of eye-splitting sparklers. It was John. So that was it! John had made the shadow run away. Was he more powerful than the shadow?

"John — " I started to say, when a loud crash and another outburst came from the storage room.

Running to the door, I shone my light into the

farthest corner just in time to see a sneakered foot disappear around the edge of a door. Padded footsteps ran down wooden stairs.

Those stairs! They were the same ones I'd seen on the other side of the pantry door. I lurched forward but was stopped by a gentle pull on my arm. John's blurred face hovered beside mine. He seemed to be struggling to maintain his shape, anxious to tell me something.

"I'll go after them," I said. "Will you come with me?"

He shook his head, his lips opening as if they were covered with a fine gauze. I could feel his frustration.

"But we have to find out who it is!" I cried.

John stretched a hand out to me as if wanting to hold on to me, but slowly, slowly, what little colour he had whitened and stretched and dissolved. In my head, I heard a familiar gentle voice. John's voice. "Careful, danger, stay clear of. . . ." The voice shrivelled and disappeared with the last bit of light.

"I have to see who it was! I have to . . . I'll be careful, I will, I will," I cried. I couldn't tell if he'd heard me. Silence pulsed through the room.

I turned and crept quickly and silently through the attic store-room and down the stairs. My tiny flashlight was losing its strength. With a few weak flutters it died in my hand. Putting my other hand on the wall to guide me, I continued down into the pitchy gloom ahead.

Just ahead, a door slammed. From behind it came the sounds of breaking glass, the scrape and crash of an overturned chair, and a long snarling growl. These were followed by a piercing scream — the howl of an injured cat. I stumbled down to the bottom stair, put my hands out and shuffled forward until my fingertips touched the outside of the pantry door. Fumbling through the narrow crowded space, I bumped up against its other door, leading into the kitchen. I groped for the door handle and stepped into the dark room.

Chapter 21

A struggle was going on somewhere near the back door. Suddenly it was flung open, crashing against the side of a kitchen cupboard. Someone rushed through the grey rectangle into the night. Right behind it came a scrabble of nails, and a low mass lunged through the opening. Hoarse deep barks faded through the yard and down the back lane.

I groped my way across the kitchen towards the light switch but half-way there, I fell over something on the floor. The dead flashlight dropped out of my hand and rattled across the linoleum. I sat back with a cry. My other hand was touching someone's face.

"Rachel. That you?"

A long silhouette appeared in the open door frame.

"Rachel. That you?"

"The lights. By the back door. Turn them on," I gasped when I got my breath back.

"Holy cow!" Will shouted. "It's Mr. Basely! You've knocked him down!"

I scrambled to my feet, blinking in the brightness. "He — he must have tried to stop the guy that was digging around upstairs. I fell over him. He was already on the floor. Max was here, too." I looked at Will. "Did you see him outside? He was chasing the guy down the back lane."

"What guy? You mean some guy was in the attic?"

He turned abruptly and ran into the night. I leaned over Mr. Basely. Blood oozed out of a wide cut on his forehead. The crinkled eyelids tried to open and he gave a soft "Ooph" through bluish lips.

"Don't move, Mr. Basely, please don't. I'll call someone — "

Will rushed back into the kitchen followed by Max, who limped up to Mr. Basely and snuffled around his face, making little whimpery noises.

"Max is hurt, too," I said. "Poor old fella!"

"I thought you told me he couldn't see anything. He was racing down the back lane. I couldn't catch up. He almost got the guy. I think I heard a loud yelp. And when he came back, he was limping. Come and see what he tore off that creep."

"I can't . . . I'm worried about Mr. Basely. He's really hurt."

The swinging door into the hall swished open and Aunt Irene and the others crowded in.

"What on earth . . . oh, my dear lord, what's happened?" cried Gladys.

I told them quickly what had happened.

Aunt Irene ran up to Mr. Basely and knelt down beside him. After checking him over carefully, she reached over for my arm and I helped her stand up. "He's alive. Thank God. Didn't I tell you . . . *all* of you that something like this could happen? And didn't I say that we should be patrolling in twos? Didn't I? But would any of you listen? Would you? And we can't keep leaving everything up to Rachel. The girl needs more direction, I said. I should have worked harder on the other one. But Quentin put too much confidence in this child . . . and in him upstairs." She shook her finger at the ceiling, then at Mr. Basely and me. "Just look!"

The Fossils were dressed in their night clothes — Gladys in a grubby velvet robe with a big safety pin holding it closed across her narrow chest; Mitzi and Luther in identical purple pyjamas and Aunt Irene in a black silk kimono and what was that? A chin strap of some sort tied in a bow on the top of her head. Mr. Basely wore a green woollen housecoat and one tweed slipper; the other was near the door. The other Fossils were barefoot — pale feet with bulgy blue veins and bunions. Luther's hair was standing straight up in back.

Gladys shuffled farther into the room. "I told you I had a feeling," she said. "I don't know why, but I did. I wish I could remember — "

"Irene is right this time," said Luther, crouching down to touch Mr. Basely gently on the shoulder. "Quentin knew there was some danger brewing for tonight. I thought he could handle things and call when he needed help. We're useless old fools. What makes us think we can look after anyone else's welfare if we can't even look after our own?"

"Don't be silly, Luther," said Mitzi firmly. "We all agreed it was probably too soon for any real danger. We thought we had more time."

As usual, I had no idea what they were talking about. And this time, I didn't care. "Someone call an ambulance before he bleeds to death!"

"I'll do it," Will said, pushing past the Fossils towards the hall phone.

"Can't you help him?" I asked Luther. "You helped me. Can't you give him something?"

Luther shook his head. "Not for an injury like this. We'd need . . . we'd need more help. I'll go with him to the hospital. I'll take some of my elixirs to give him strength. That's all I can do."

I looked at Mr. Basely's white still face. "That's all you can do?" I stood up and shouted. "What good are you! You act like you know everything. But you're useless really, aren't you? You'll just let him lie here and die. You're all just plain *useless*!"

The Fossils looked at each other in shock. Luther nodded. "You're right. We *are* useless. Right now, our powers are limited, but not for long." He looked at me hard. "We hate not being able to help him, Rachel. He's our friend."

In my confusion and shame I turned away and

164

crouched down beside Mr. Basely. I had no right to yell at them. I couldn't help, either.

"What the hell's going on?" Bridgette appeared, stifling a yawn and scratching her stomach through a flannel nightgown. Her small eyes widened when she saw Mr. Basely. "God, now what?"

"Someone was searching the attic again, in the store-room. He ran down here and Max chased him down the street," I said.

"What's this?" asked Mitzi. She picked up the thing that Will had taken from Max. She examined it closely. "Why, it's a chunk of leather. Torn off a jacket. With teeth marks on it."

I looked up from dabbing Mr. Basely's head with a dishcloth. "Will said Max tore it off the guy he was chasing."

"There's a button attached to it. I've seen it somewhere before," she said. "Who has one like it?"

I got to my feet and looked at it. "Roger! I knew it was him. I shone my flashlight on him. It had to be him."

"Roger?" said Bridgette blinking slowly, her mouth hanging open. Then quick as a snake, she turned on me. "Hey, don't be so sure, kid. God, you're really out to get me, aren't you? You didn't see anything," she sneered, but it was a feeble sneer. Her eyes looked uneasy, the wide-eyed gaze going from me to the button and back again.

"It was him, all right. That's a piece of his jacket."

"You little liar!" she squealed. "First you say

165

it's me up there and then you say it's my boy-friend. Well, I'll tell you — "

I shook the piece of leather in her face. "It's his. See? Look at this button. It's in the shape of a half-moon. Recognize it now?"

Bridgette took the piece of leather, stared at it, then at Max lying beside his master.

"Okay. So? Big deal. Maybe Roger was out-side. Going for a walk, innocent like, and this stupid dog chases him."

"No!" I said firmly. "I saw that jacket button upstairs tonight. It was him. I'd swear it."

Bridgette dropped the piece of leather as if it burned her fingertips and stepped back. "He-promised-me-he-wouldn't-hurt-anyone," she mumbled, her words slurred together.

"What was that, Bridgette?" Aunt Irene demanded.

Bridgette, her eyes almost popping out of her head by then, shouted, "He promised if I gave him a key, he'd use it only once! But he didn't give it back. He said he'd lost it. He said there was great stuff to sell up there in the storage room. Then we'd get a place of our own. *He promised!*"

"Oh, Bridgette, how could you, dear?" asked Gladys, touching Bridgette's arm.

"How? How? It's all your fault," Bridgette screamed. "If you'd given me money when I asked, I'd be long gone. But no! You had to keep hold of it!"

Gladys shook her head sadly. "I told you, dear. I have no money. None."

"You're lying. You all have money. Hidden

166

somewhere. Roger said you'd probably stashed it upstairs."

"Well, he fooled you good, didn't he?" said Luther. "We should have been more suspicious. But we know what he's really after now. Go to bed, you silly girl. But first take a good look at what that creature did to our friend. And you helped him."

"No, I didn't! No, I didn't!" Bridgette clutched the front of her nightgown with both hands. "He said he wouldn't hurt anyone! He *promised*!" With a long open-mouthed wail she ran out of the room.

Luther knelt beside Mr. Basely. I'd put a clean dishcloth over the cut.

"Shouldn't we call the police? I could tell Will to call them," I whispered.

"There's no need for them yet," he said. "Besides, in this case, they couldn't do anything. We know who it is. And why he's here."

"Who?" I asked. "But what does Roger — "

"The ambulance is on its way," Will said, running back into the room. "It took me ages to get through. I think the lines were crossed or something. They said it would be fifteen minutes or so."

Mitzi put a fingertip to her mouth. "Cripes, Luther, you'd better get changed. You'll want to go along. Don't forget your medicines. And Quentin will need some things packed. Let's go, people."

The three women turned and made for the door, bumping into each other and crowding through it.

167

"I'll wait outside for the ambulance and show them where to come," said Will.

"Good boy," Luther said. "What is he doing here at this time of night? Never mind. I was young once, too. Now look, Rachel, this is what I want you to do. I've got to go and get changed. I want you to put pressure on this folded cloth on his forehead. Not too hard, just enough to keep down the bleeding. He won't bleed to death. Forehead cuts always bleed a lot. Can you do that?"

I nodded and he left with the others. I looked down at Mr. Basely. I could see the veins across his temples, like dark blue lines under an onion skin. The blood was darkening in his white hair. I tried to control my wobbly chin and tear-squeezed throat. All I seemed to do was fight off tears these days.

"Irene was right," said a thin voice.

"Mr. Basely? Oh, Mr. Basely," I said softly, my tears dropping on his face.

"Yes," he said, "she was right. My fault entirely. It's time you knew. So much potential. But we could lose it. We need to talk to John. He must know it by now." He tried to sit up, but sank back with a deep sigh. "Too damn old. Too slow and fussy." He closed his eyes. "Your aunt must tell you. But she must be careful. It's my fault. We wasted too much time hoping. But you are so vulnerable, you couldn't know too soon."

What was he trying to say? "John? You know John?" I asked. "But I've seen him, Mr. Basely."

He opened his eyes wide. "Have you? Irene

168

said she thought you had. That's splendid. He'll help you if you need him. But not too often. He's weakening, growing tired. Poor boy. Like all of us, I suppose, until you came to us."

"He was up there tonight. He chased them away."

"Them?" He looked alarmed.

"Yes. Roger and . . . and . . ."

He clutched my arm.

"And a big black shadow. Like . . . like a big bat or a bird," I said.

A whooping siren cut through the still cold air outside.

Mr. Basely's hand tightened. "I'll speak to Irene. Be careful. Stay close to someone all the time . . . I'll be home tomorrow and we'll begin." His grip loosened.

"I'll be okay. And don't worry, I'll look after Max, Mr. Basely. Mr. Basely?"

He was lying so still, I became really frightened. The piercing jangle of the doorbell echoed down the hall.

"Mr. Basely. Hang on. They're here," I sobbed. "Hang on."

His pale lips opened. "I'll be fine. Luther will fix me up. Don't worry, love."

He didn't look fine. He looked as if he had no blood left in his body. He looked like he was dying. What would I do if he died? What more was going to happen?

Chapter 22

I waited with Will and the others on the front porch until the ambulance pulled away with a choking wail.

"Quentin will be fine, kiddo," said Mitzi. She'd wiped her eyes over and over with the same soggy tissue and they were red and puffy. Gladys and Aunt Irene were holding hands, their creased faces as pale as dust, with matching hollow eyes.

"He . . . Mr. Basely said you had something really important to tell me," I said. "Can you tell me now?"

Aunt Irene reached out with a shaky hand. It was cold. She pulled me near and touched my cheek. "I can't. Not tonight. I'm too drained. I have to consult with Mitzi and Gladys. And we have to find out how Quentin is first. It must be done right. And we need our sleep if things are going to happen tomorrow as Quentin hopes. Tomorrow. Yes, tomorrow." Her voice trailed off.

"But what if this creep breaks in again tonight?" Will demanded.

"I don't think he will," I said. "John will look after me, won't he?" The synchronized intake of breath almost made me laugh for the first time that night. "Don't worry. Mr. Basely knows I've seen him."

Aunt Irene, Mitzi and Gladys circled me.

"There's one thing we've got to know, kiddo," said Mitzi. "Was there someone . . . ummmm . . . other . . . well . . . person, I guess you might say — was there someone else with this Roger tonight?"

"Yes."

"Who?" asked Will. "You mean John?"

"No. It was that shadow I told you about, Will. The big winged shadow. It was in the store-room with Roger. It tried to . . ." I looked at the worried faces around me, "to suffocate me, I think." I shivered.

"Jeez!" was all that Will could manage.

The women moved in closer, jostling into each other in their anxiety.

"And you've seen this shadow before?" Aunt Irene demanded.

I nodded.

"Oooo! He's found us! Rachel brought him here. It worked! I knew it! I saw him the other day. I can't remember — could it have been? No, still, I did see him! Oooo," cried Gladys, looking over her shoulder. "It is *him*, isn't it?"

"It would seem so. Pull yourself together, Gladys," snapped Aunt Irene, looking more like her old self. "Well, it's time. Inevitable. Don't worry, Rachel dear, we don't believe he — er — this shadow can really harm you at this time. Now, what to do? Rachel, you can look after Max. Take Will with you. The three of us have work to do. We'll lock all the doors leading upstairs. Keep Max close by. He can set up an alarm if he senses anything amiss. Will, after you've helped Rachel, you go off home. Rachel will sleep with me tonight."

"No way am I going anywhere," Will said. "I'll stay in Rachel's room with Max."

"But what about your parents?" she asked.

"I'll zip back there in the morning. They sleep in on weekends. They won't know I was gone."

"I don't know . . ." said Aunt Irene. "They've probably heard the ambulance. Maybe they've checked your room."

"Nah. My dad could sleep through a hurricane. And my mom sleeps through his snoring. You'll have a tough time throwing me out."

Aunt Irene nodded. " 'Bravery never goes out of fashion.' "

Will looked pleased. Then he frowned. "I'm not brave. I've never been brave."

Mitzi laughed. "Maybe brave just means crazy, eh? We're all crazy in this house."

"I'm not missing out, either," I said. "Max and Will and I can guard the attic. Just in case John wants to talk to me. He won't come if I'm not there."

"I don't know, Rachel," said Mitzi. "Seems a bit risky you being up there."

"But Mr. Basely said as long as I had another person with me I'd be okay. And Max is a good watch-dog. He can bark and bark and you can come running," I said.

Aunt Irene, to my surprise, was the first to give in again. "Well, you'll have to face things like this sooner or later. There's some extra blankets in the linen closet upstairs, Rachel. Come, ladies, let's go batten down the hatches. Call if you need us, you two."

Max was still in the kitchen lying near the small puddle of Mr. Basely's blood. When Will and I walked in, he growled softly and tried to stand, but groaned deeply and sank back to the floor.

"That creep must have kicked him good," Will said. "We'll have to take him to the vet if it isn't better soon, huh? I'll get a rag or something to clean up the mess."

I leaned over Max and patted his head and felt his injured leg. His small agate eyes looked up at me knowingly, carefully. He slumped to one side and closed his eyes.

"Max. Did I hurt you, boy?"

His tail thumped the floor and he growled softly before slowly standing up on his great bowed legs. We grinned at each other and I rubbed his ears.

The phone on the kitchen wall rang. I lunged for it and gasped, "Yes?" into the receiver. Expecting Luther's voice, I was surprised by the confused crackle of static and what sounded like distant voices.

"Hello?" I said loudly.

"Rachel?" a voice asked, barely recognizable through the sputtering and hissing of the static and other voices.

"Dad?" I shouted. "Dad, is that you?"

"We have a bad line," he shouted back. "Thank goodness it's you! Can . . . hear . . . me?"

"A little bit," I shouted back. "Can you call again?"

"Can't. Just on my way . . . and the roads are awful . . . rain . . . mud . . . so I thought I'd call. Rachel are . . . okay?"

Another voice, a coarse heckling voice, was growing louder. I couldn't make out what it was saying.

"Dad," I yelled into the receiver, "I need you to come home. Please?"

". . . honey. Long trip . . . damn engine trouble . . . go back, but . . . hope to see . . . soon — "

The heckling voice was joined by more voices that laughed and shouted but without words, without any sense at all.

"Good to hear . . . voice, honey. I was worried . . . be there before . . . know it." Dad shouted. "Gotta go, babe."

"Dad! Come home. I need you, please!" I cried, but the line had gone dead. I banged it against the wall and burst into tears.

Chapter 23

Will found me huddled against the wall, the receiver still in my hands, bawling with great sobbing gulps that soaked the front of my sweater. Between hiccups, I told him what had happened. He sat on the floor beside me, one arm around my shoulder, and patted my back until I stopped. Sometimes he does know when to keep his mouth shut.

A half hour later, Max and Will and I were settled upstairs for what was left of the night. My swollen eyes felt like poached eggs. The old dog settled down with a few painful grunts and wheezes on an extra blanket at the foot of the bed. Will dragged the two armchairs together to create a makeshift bed and curled his lanky form into the small space with pretend echoes of Max's discomfort. When I turned the light out, I heard low cursing and then a loud thump.

"Why not just sleep on the floor?" I asked. "Wouldn't that be easier?"

"Where do you think I am at this moment? Hey, you got an extra pillow?"

I threw him one. Soon the only sounds were the muffled snores of the dog.

"Rach?"

"Yeah?"

"Do you think John's with us now?"

I closed my eyes. "Yeah, I do."

I could almost hear Will's eyelids clicking open and shut in the dark. "Rach?"

"Yes?"

"I'm not sure I like that idea. Even if he is a good guy. You know, you really haven't told me what happened here tonight."

"The bad guys were here and John helped get rid of them. He'd do it again in a minute. We'll be okay." I hoped he didn't hear the doubt in my voice. I remembered how John had had difficulty holding his light and shape, and my heart took a little jump of fear. Would he be able to come back soon if we needed him? "He's tired," I continued. "But I think he's here."

"Great," he muttered. "Just dandy."

"What worries me is Dad," I said. "I wish I could have told him what's happening. It's as if the Fossils are my family now and Dad is a stranger or something. Do you think he might have heard me when I asked him to get back quick?"

"I bet he did," Will answered. "But sometimes parents are pretty involved in what they're doing, you know?"

176

"Your parents don't seem like that," I said.

"Perfect they ain't," he said. "My dad's into his teaching and his pictures. Sometimes he doesn't leave enough time just to talk — and my mom, well, sometimes I think she wishes I was a *real* problem kid so she could deal with it, you know? Help me over the hurdles." He sighed.

"Just be glad they're both there," I said, trying hard not to sound bitter.

"Sorry." He yawned. "So, what's your aunt going to tell you tomorrow, I wonder?"

I watched the shadow of the big oak outside move up and down across the wall. "That's one more thing I don't know."

"I wish I could be there. You don't suppose they're witches or something, do you? I mean with Luther's bottles of stuff and cat men and shadows and all that?"

"Will, please," I begged. "In a few hours I'll know. And I'm not all that sure I want to know."

"Except that you're part of the main event," he said, "and we don't even know what it is. Jeez, it's so exhausting."

His sigh turned into a soft burbling snore. It was hard to tell him and Max apart.

"Boy," I muttered. "I'll never get to sleep now." In a few minutes I'd joined them.

The next morning, Will woke me up. By poking my shoulder. Very romantic. "Hey. Sleepyhead. I gotta get home. You awake?"

I groped for my glasses and blinked at him sleepily.

"My folks'll be up soon," he continued. "And you've got to get ready to talk to your aunt."

I sat up. "Right. Don't want to miss that." I chewed at my bottom lip. "But what about Mr. Basely? I should see him."

"They won't let you near the hospital until this afternoon. Anyway, maybe your aunt's heard. Hurry up. You've got to talk to her."

"You go home. I'll come over as soon as I'm done."

"So . . . you okay alone for a bit?" he asked. "You sure you don't want me to stay?"

"I'm sure. I'll see you in a half hour. I've got Max."

"Right. See you later then." He leaned over and patted my head. Well, patted the top of the red Brillo pad my hair always turns into during the night. "I'd kiss you, but I'd melt your face with morning breath," he said. "However, when all this is over, scientifically speaking, I would quite like to explore the possibilities of . . ." he paused, dramatically, ". . . The Kiss."

I threw my pillow at him but he dodged and ran down the stairs. I stretched again and smiled. Imagine that. Me. Getting soppy over a boy. Max shoved his face into mine. He champed his jaws and backed towards the stairs, then came back to snuffle my hand. I patted his head. "You're right, boy. Let's go." I put on my housecoat and helped Max downstairs. He followed me down the hall, his big head bumping the backs of my legs with friendly nudges.

A quick knock on Aunt Irene's door was answered with a curt, "Enter."

I'd never seen inside her bedroom. "Hey, this

is nice," I said, looking around at the big four-poster bed, the chintz curtains and soft wool rugs. It smelled good in the room, like spring lilacs.

She was sitting up in bed, a cup of tea in one hand and what looked like a plain rye-crisp in the other. A pink shawl covered her shoulders and her black and silver hair fell over it.

"You must have been really pretty," I blurted out, and immediately covered my mouth. "Gosh, sorry."

Aunt Irene smiled. "Don't be sorry. And I was. Very pretty. Mr. Basely will be coming home this morning. Isn't that good news? Remember my dear, 'The cunning seldom gain their ends: the wise are never without friends.' He is a very wise friend. And of course, he is anxious that you be taken good care of."

"When can I see him?" I asked.

"This afternoon, dear. After he's settled. We have to have a council meeting of tenants, so to speak." She waved her biscuit in the air. "We want you to attend. We have to prepare, you see."

"For what?" I asked.

She sat forward. "I — I, dear me, where to begin . . ."

"Just answer me this," I said. "Am I somehow the . . . the reason all this is going on? Did I cause it?"

"In a way, yes. You. And John and . . . you're so young . . . I wish . . ." Here she smiled, "But then wishes aren't much use to us now, are

179

they?" She smoothed her cover and twiddled her biscuit in the air.

"What are you talking about?" I was getting impatient.

"I hate to see you involved, but, well, we need you now and that's all there is to it," she muttered, almost to herself.

"Will I have to do something, something to — stop all this?"

She looked at me suddenly with a look that reminded me of Dad after Joanna left, a look that flashed a deep unspoken pain. "I should have known you'd sense the danger," she whispered.

I knew then that it wasn't just up to Aunt Irene and the Fossils to decide whether I would be a part of things. I had a feeling that things had already been decided by others outside their little circle.

"Wh-what do I have to do?" I asked.

She sighed. "Sit down, Rachel. I've got something to say to you."

She put her cup and biscuit on the little table beside her and patted the side of her bed. I sat down near her. We smiled tentatively at each other, but then she frowned and muttered, "This is so awkward, Rachel dear. You're a modern young woman, and I'm about to tell you something quite fantastic. You'll really think I'm dotty if I tell you who we really are — by we I mean me, Mr. Basely, Mitzi, Luther . . . and yes, even little Gladys — although she's only an honorary member, you might say." She peered at me intently as if to gauge whether I was already lining her up as a crackpot.

"A member of what?" I asked. "Are you all witches or something like that?"

Aunt Irene looked startled and then she laughed — a short sharp bark. "Oh dear me, no! Whatever gave you that idea. Witches?" She laughed again. "Hah! That's a good one. Maybe you are ready. Let me see, how can I explain it all without getting myself and you all muddled up."

She cleared her throat. "Our people started with a man named Peadair Griogair. That's Gaelic for Peter Gregor. His name means watcher of the — er — stone. Centuries ago, this Peter Gregor gathered together a small band of people with special talents. They formed a small community, the Gregor Clan, and they lived in Scotland as farmers and skilled craftsmen and such like. They lived in complete harmony with nature and with nearby villages." She leaned towards me and tapped my arm. "But these villagers didn't know that that Gregor Clan or at least many of them had special gifts. Only a few outsiders — some in high office — knew about the Gregor Clan's powers."

"Powers?" I asked. "Like what?"

Aunt Irene looked confused. "I'm not sure I'm supposed to tell you all of this . . . but well, some of them could tell the future, for instance, and others could see events happening miles away — what people now call second sight."

I felt my mind become very still. Of course. That's what I had. Second sight. "Am I one of the special people?" I asked, but I already knew the answer.

She nodded. "A direct descendant."

A direct descendant! "Were they sort of a secret group then?" I asked.

"The last thing these people were was evil," she said. "But superstition being what it was and is, the Gregor Clan knew that their powers couldn't be explained — and what can't be explained is often seen as dangerous, perhaps evil. So it was kept secret, except from the few who appreciated their skills — certain scholars, teachers and those in power that the clan were loyal to."

"They were pretty good people, then?" I asked.

"On the whole, yes. They believed in behaving valiantly and fairly to all." She reached over and poured herself more tea. "But human nature being what it is, a few people of this group would sometimes try to use their powers for bad reasons. To steal from the outsiders or to make themselves richer and more powerful. So the little community voted to have a special group to watch over the others, to make sure that they only use their powers for good. This group of people was called a Guardian Circle." She grimaced. "That, believe it or not, is what we are in this house."

"So that's what you are," I breathed. "A Guardian Circle."

"Yes," said Aunt Irene. "Into the twentieth century in one simple sentence."

"And I'm one of your group?"

"Yes. And we're here to watch over you and John."

"John?"

"We've been afraid to tell you too much. As a 'sensitive,' and a young, untested one at that, we've been afraid to place you in danger. You didn't know us and we didn't know you. You were angry, unhappy. We had to gain your trust." She shook her head. "Didn't do very well, did we?"

"You sound awfully important," I said.

Aunt Irene smiled sadly and squeezed my hand before letting it go. "The only difference between us and other human beings is that many of us have a little magic inside us — some more powerful than others. We might have been important once — the world is very big now . . ."

"What happened to the clan?"

"Well, dear, the land that the Gregors lived on had belonged to a wealthy, titled family since the times of Elizabeth I. Our clan had been allowed to live there — for services rendered, you might say. But in 1863 a young upstart became the new lord, or laird as it's known in Scotland. His ancestors had always respected the Gregors and their abilities, and they had the clan's loyalty. But this new laird was a scientific man, he said. He'd travelled the world and he wanted to turn the land into one huge farm for a bigger profit. I think he was jealous of our small group and I think deep down very afraid of us. Many of the smaller farmers had already been pushed off the land years before during the land enclosures — by greedy landowners who wanted richer, larger farms. The young laird used the same excuse. We had to go."

"Where?"

"The cities and villages were already overpopulated. The clan split up, going to different countries to find work. In 1865 a small band landed at Nova Scotia. The leader was a woman named Mairghread Gregor. She was a direct descendant of Peter Gregor."

"And was she special, too?" I asked.

"Oh, my, yes. She watched over and cared for her small group. Mairghread's skills got them through the tough times. And they managed. Some of the younger ones had been quite well educated by this time. A few became teachers. Several shopkeepers. Others gradually bought farms. Mairghread had one great disappointment in her life, however, that couldn't be remedied."

"What?" I barely breathed.

"Her son, Dunstan, had refused to come with her when she left the Old Country. He was already living in England. Mairghread had sent him to be educated at Oxford so that he would return and become one of the teachers. He liked the high living he'd fallen into. He didn't want to return to the clan, especially in a raw new world. As time went on, he used his powers more and more to further himself. He wanted fame. And he was greedy for wealth. He became known as a man who could tell people what their futures held — he could do all sorts of magical things, including talking to the dead. People came to him from all over to communicate with loved ones who'd passed on. This was a skill to be used only in extraordinary circumstances and

184

he abused it time and time again. Finally word came to Mairghread that Dunstan was blackmailing people with facts he'd picked up using his powers.

"When she heard about this in Canadá, she cut off all communication with him, disowned him. He didn't like that, because he wanted to make sure that when she died, she'd hand over . . ." Aunt Irene looked around.

"What?" I asked.

Aunt Irene leaned forward and mouthed the words, "The Gregor Stone."

"The Stone?" I asked. "What — "

"Ssssh!" sprayed Aunt Irene, her eyes darting in all directions.

"But — "

"Rachel, please!" she said clutching her chest. "Don't say it out loud."

"Okay, okay, I won't," I said, then dropped to a whisper, "but what is it?"

Her hands fluttered in the air. "We'll tell you about it when we all get together. Suffice it to say that . . . it . . . was passed on to Mairghread's only daughter, Bethia. And she, in turn, passed it on to her own son. It has been missing ever since he died. We know now that he hid it from his uncle Dunstan. You see, her son didn't believe the . . . of its powers . . . and he didn't try to learn the old ways. He viewed himself as a modern man and didn't believe in what he called superstitious nonsense. Just before he died, he realized how wrong he was and he hid the . . . it . . . and now we have to find it before Dunstan Gregor does."

"Dunstan? *That* Dunstan?" I cried. "How can he still be alive?"

Aunt Irene leaned over and grabbed my arm. "He's not! That's what frightens us so. He — his wicked spirit has tracked us down. He wants to take over the powers of the . . . you-know-what. He needs it."

"How — where did he die?" My head was reeling with all the information.

She sat back and said with grim satisfaction, "He was murdered. By one of his so-called friends. In 1890. Not long after his mother died."

"Murdered!"

"I suppose he blackmailed one too many people." Aunt Irene fell back onto her pillows. "I'm afraid that's all I can tell you. There are one or two very important things more, but I must wait until we are gathered so that we will have strength in numbers when the complete story comes out. What you don't understand . . ." She held up one hand when I made to argue. "Please, Rachel dear, our little Guardian Circle is very fragile. And the more we tell you, the more vulnerable we become. Please be patient. Soon you'll know everything." She turned her head on the pillow and looked closely at my face. "You'll have a very important decision to make, little one. You are our only hope now."

Chapter 24

When I rang Will's doorbell, I was expecting him to answer it. My smile slipped off my face and fell on the doorstep between his mother and me.

"Rachel. Will just called down that this must be you. He's just getting up, lazy kid. Come on in, have you eaten?"

Without thinking, I shook my head. I looked desperately at the stairs leading up to the second floor. Where was he? It was obvious he'd been able to sneak in and fool his parents this morning but he should have been on the look-out for me.

"Will!" she called. "Rachel's here!" She looked at me and smiled an isn't-this-cute-you-and-my-son-together kind of smile. This woman never gave up.

She made me sit down in the kitchen and plunked a stack of pancakes in front of me, apologizing all the while that they were a new apple-fritter recipe, so might not be what I was used to. I couldn't think of how to refuse them. I wanted to check for zucchini, but she shoved butter and syrup at me and shouted through the door for Will to get a move on, breakfast was ready.

The fritters weren't too bad, actually, certainly better than anything Gladys had invented. And I was really hungry. In fact, I felt strangely in control for the first time since I'd arrived on this street. I thought of Aunt Irene and smiled to myself. She needed *me*. So did the others. I belonged to an old line of very special people. I wasn't going crazy! And I finally had a reason for the Warnings and the dreams.

I became aware that Will's mom had sat down at the table and was watching me stuff my face. I swallowed hard and took a smaller bite the next time.

"So, Rachel — " she began. Thank goodness Will walked in just in time. She pointed to the oven. "In there. And bring Rachel some more bacon. It's nice to see a girl with a good appetite." I wondered if syrup was running down my chin. I wiped my mouth carefully.

Will sat down and dug in, glancing back and forth between us.

"Aren't you going to say hello to Rachel?" his mother asked.

"Sure," said Will, grinning. "Hello, Rachel. Did you have a good night's sleep?"

"Just fine," I said in a sweet voice. "Did you?"

"Yes, I did. How about you, mother dear? Did you?"

She narrowed her eyes. "Yes, I did, thank you."

She continued to hover for awhile, but it got so quiet that she finally took the hint, and stood up with a "Well, I'd better — "

Mr. Lennox poked his head around the corner. "Oh, hi there, Rachel. Come on, Sandy. Move it."

"We're going for a drive. Pictures," she said meaningfully, pointing at the cameras over Mr. Lennox's shoulders. "Want to come?"

"Leave the kids alone, Sandy. Let's go." He winked at us.

We waited until we heard the car start up in the drive.

Will lunged forward over the table. "Well?"

I took a deep breath and told him everything Aunt Irene had told me. When I was done, he sat very still, staring at the puddle of syrup on his plate.

"You're not kidding, are you," he said. "Not putting me on, I mean."

"Will!"

"Yeah, I know what you said, just let me wrap it once more around my brain and see if I can soak it all up." I waited. "Cripes, Rachel, this scares me. She says this guy, this shadow thing, is after some stone, but she doesn't really say anything about where it is!"

"She said I'd find out later today. I guess John will tell them somehow. John!" I slapped my forehead. "I forgot to ask Aunt Irene where John fits into the story!"

"You can find out later." He ran his hand through his hair. "I remember asking you who are *they*. Now, I'm looking at you and I'm wondering, who are *you*? Do you feel any different?"

"I feel the same . . . and yet, different, you know? That's how she made me feel. Special."

"I wonder if you should leave that house for a while. Think things through. It's all happening so fast."

I shook my head. "Aunt Irene said things were at a crisis point. If I don't help the Fossils, I don't know what will happen to them. This shadow — it's bad, hateful. It used to be Dunstan Gregor — it is Dunstan Gregor." I remembered the shadow and shivered. "Look, I have to get back, as soon as Mr. Basely comes home. They're going to tell me all the details then. Will you come too?"

He nodded. "Yeah, listen, Rachel, I — "

The front door banged open. "It's just me," yodelled Mrs. Lennox. "I forgot my ear-muffs. By the way, Rachel," she added, standing in the doorway, "I just saw two of the old fellows from your place. They arrived in a taxi. One of them has a bandage on his head. Has something happened?"

"They're back?" I said, standing up quickly and scraping the chair back.

"Mr. Basely bumped his head on an open cupboard door," Will said to his mother, who looked like she might start on a pot of Good Samaritan soup. "He just went in for observation and

190

stitches. He's okay. Isn't he, Rach. Rachel?"

I was shoving my arms in my jacket. "Huh? Yeah. He's okay."

"Well . . . I wonder — " Mrs. Lennox began.

"Are you coming?" Mr. Lennox bellowed from the front door.

"Oh dear. I did promise your dad. We'll be late. We're stopping in on friends out by Portage la Prairie for coffee. We'll be home by dinner," she said. I watched her fuss. Maybe Mrs. Lennox wasn't so bad after all. She sure was a lot different than Joanna. Joanna wouldn't have cared less about an injured old man. I guess some people care and some don't. Maybe Joanna just didn't know how to care for anyone else. Maybe no one showed her how. Anyways, I've accepted that as the explanation, for now.

A blast of the car horn made Mrs. Lennox move. "Oh darn. See you later, kids."

We stood at the front door and watched her talk rapidly to Mr. Lennox. She pointed to 135. He shook his head and it looked like he might be shouting. Then she nodded and touched his arm. He backed the car out and they were gone.

"Whew! I thought she would never leave," breathed Will. "I guess we'd better make tracks over there, eh?"

"Yeah," I whispered. "Let's go."

When we walked in the back door of 135, Bridgette was sitting at the table, smoking a cigarette, a tattered cloth suitcase on the floor beside her. Will and I watched her warily as we headed towards the door leading into the hall.

"You don't need to worry," she growled. "He

191

ain't here. You've lost me the only boyfriend I'll probably ever have." She ground the butt into the saucer and glanced at us from under her greasy bangs. "Not that I'd want him after what he did. But old Basely'll be okay. So I'm not worried or nothin'."

The drooping figure at the table reminded me of some of the feelings I'd had — knowing nobody wants you and being angry and hurt. "What's with the suitcase?" I asked. "You're not leaving, are you?"

"Huh! As if you care," said Bridgette, but she didn't put much poison into it. "Mr. Dawson and his wife are giving me a room at their place. They don't have no family — no kids or nothin'. I — I guess I was pretty upset this morning when I went in to help set the dough." She eyed us defiantly. "They think you're all a bunch of weirdos. Hey, don't bother opening your yap, kid, I never told them about him in the attic."

"You'll probably be a lot — you know — happier at the bakery," I said. "And I'm sure Mr. Basely will be back to normal in no time."

I couldn't believe it. Bridgette's eyes actually filled with tears. "Do you really think so? I'd hate . . . well . . . I wouldn't want to've . . ."

"Yeah, I know," I said. "Maybe I'll see you at the bakery one day."

Bridgette searched in her plastic purse, took out another cigarette and lit up. "Mr. Dawson'll be here pretty soon. You better get in there. They've been looking for you."

"Come on, Rachel," said Will, pushing open the swinging door.

I started to follow, but I stopped when Bridgette said, "Hey, kid."

"Yeah?"

"Look . . . uh . . . I know you didn't squeal on me after the attic was wrecked, okay?"

I nodded. "Okay."

"See you."

I smiled. "Yeah, I'll come and get some doughnuts some time."

Bridgette tapped her ash into the saucer and waved me away, but I was sure I saw the hint of a sad smile on her thin lips.

Chapter 25

Will and I were half-way down the hall when Aunt Irene's head appeared under the edge of the staircase.

"Finally here she is!" she cried. She marched towards us followed by Mitzi, Luther and Gladys.

Gladys hugged me. "We've been waiting for you. Mr. Basely's home! Isn't that lovely?"

"But he's been warned to take it easy," Aunt Irene added. "And we have to . . ." She noticed Will. "Dear me, yes. I know it's wrong to 'speed a guest who does not want to go,' but in this case, Will, I think you'd better get on home. Come along, Rachel."

"No," I said firmly. "Will stays. He knows everything anyway."

"What do you mean?" asked Aunt Irene.

"How could he know? What could he possibly know? Did you tell him?"

"Never mind, Irenie," said Mitzi. "He can't know *everything*. Let him stay. He has very good emanations. A very good aura. Right, Luther? He can be made to forget later, if . . . you know."

"What does *that* mean?" Will asked, looking worried.

Luther bared his yellow teeth. "Not to worry, son. We know you wouldn't let Rachel down. A lot like you and me once, eh, Mitzi my pet?"

The tips of Will's ears flared red. "I'd never let her down."

"Exactly," said Luther. "So let's get with it."

We all crowded into Mr. Basely's study. He was sitting in a big leather chair wrapped in a moth-eaten Bay blanket. I ran over to him and stood close to the arm of the chair. He reached out from under the blanket and gripped my arm near the elbow. We smiled widely at each other. Will dragged a chair over and I sat down beside Mr. Basely.

"Now?" asked Aunt Irene, once everyone was seated.

Mr. Basely and the others nodded. "Yes, now," he said. "We've waited far too long for this." He reached out. His hand felt smooth and dry, like a fine leather glove. "Let's hope we're not too weak and flabby to be of any help."

Aunt Irene bristled. "I prefer to think we're on the threshold of a whole new age of power."

Luther shrugged. "If we can't find the door, how can we cross the threshold, Irenie? We're fumbling in the dark."

"Please, let's not be downhearted," pleaded Gladys. "It's so upsetting."

"Gladys is quite right," said Mr. Basely. "So let's begin. Now. Who would like to do the honours? True confessions time, Rachel. Oh, Irene, please don't look like that. A little light-heartedness never went wrong. There'll be time enough for seriousness."

"Why don't you begin, then, Quentin?" said Mitzi. "Or Irenie? It doesn't matter. Does it?"

"No, no," said Aunt Irene with a sniff. "I've said quite enough already, I think."

"Even so — " offered Mr. Basely.

I interrupted them. "Look, Aunt Irene told me quite a bit. But there were some things she wouldn't answer. Maybe if I asked some questions, whoever knows the answer could tell me."

"Good enough, kiddo," said Luther, "quiz away."

"Well . . ." I began, "I know you are a Guardian Circle. I know where the idea came from. And how everything began, sort of. Aunt Irene said I was a direct descendant of the special group that came from Scotland to Canada over a hundred years ago. But how direct? She told me about Mairghread and her kids, Bethia and Dunstan. But they were all Gregors. I'm not a Gregor."

"Well, yes, you are," Mr. Basely said. "When Bethia married, she married a man from her own community. His name was Thomas MacCaw. Usually, in the Gregor family, the name Gregor was kept, be it woman or man that married. But Bethia chose to take her husband's name, I think, to avoid any connection with her rotter of a brother. Thomas and Bethia were your great-great grandparents."

"That's incredible. You mean my family — is . . . was — "

"Yes. The Gregors," said Mr. Basely.

"Then the one you're all worried about, this Dunstan guy, is Rachel's uncle with a couple of greats added on," Will said.

"Exactly right," said Mitzi.

"But what about John," I said. "In the attic? Who's he?"

Aunt Irene spoke up. "John is Bethia and Thomas's son, Rachel. John MacCaw. Your great-grandfather and the protector of the — er — the . . ."

"We're all here," Luther said. "You can say it."

"Right," said Mr. Basely. "He was the last of the Gregors to be the Protector of the Gregor Stone. Until now, that is." He smiled at me.

"The Stone!" I said to Will. "It's just hit me. That's what John meant by writing the word stone when we used the ouija." The Fossils looked blank, but I didn't bother explaining. "But what does this Stone do? Why does Dunstan Gregor want it so badly?"

"It is a part of an ancient Stone used by the Gregors to enhance their powers," said Mr. Basely. "When they left Scotland, they saw it as an opportunity to ensure a balance in the world — to try to maintain peace and harmony — or even restore it where it had been lost. Each group took a small piece of the stone."

"But why? What does it do?" I insisted.

"It helps us link into the time streams, past and future, and it strengthens our personal abilities, so to speak. So we can prepare. So that we can effect change, even if it is a small change." Mr. Basely put the tips of his fingers together.

"And John wants me to have it?" I asked.

"He's been waiting. To pass on the Gregor Stone to the next Protector."

"And Dunstan Gregor is here, too, isn't he?" I whispered.

"But Dunstan feels he was cheated out of it by his sister," said Irene, "and he . . ." She looked helplessly at Mr. Basely.

Mr. Basely cleared his throat. "What your dear aunt is having difficulty telling you is . . ." he wriggled in his seat, "is that we think he not only wants the Stone, he wants you as well."

Will stood up. "You mean kill her?"

"No. No. Sit down, sit down. She'd be no good to him that way. No, he wants her on *this* side. He wants to control both her and the Stone in our world. We, as a Guardian Circle, cannot allow that, of course." He cleared his throat again and the other Fossils shifted uneasily in their seats. "But of course, Rachel has to make up her mind to help us fight him."

"And if I don't then I suppose he'll fight you and John and win and take the Stone," I said. "But how can he? It isn't his."

"When Bethia received the Stone from her mother, Dunstan was wild with anger. He said he was the oldest and he had as many powers as she did. But she refused. Even after he died,

198

he chased after poor Bethia, but she was clever, too. She wouldn't be tricked out of it. She gave it to her son John when she knew she was about to die. John accepted it, very reluctantly. I don't think he believed in it at that time, either. To the amazement of his tiny community, he disappeared with it. He came to Winnipeg. He married and had a son. But he became very ill with TB soon after. His mother had warned him about his uncle and now he understood. He was being haunted by this monster and realized the danger to his young son. So he hid the Stone and sent his wife and son to England to live with her family. He moved into this house with his friend, Dr. Leach, who looked after him until he died."

"Why didn't John's son become the Protector?"

Aunt Irene said, "As a member of Thomas MacCaw's family and one of the Guardians, I was asked to find John's son. We knew nothing about John's wife or her family. But finally, after many years, I found him." Her eyes looked pained. "The boy's name was Richard MacCaw. But he wasn't a boy any more. He'd become a wealthy businessman who'd married late in life — wife came from a long line of British landowners. He was celebrating the birth of his own son. It was in 1946. I tried to talk to Richard, but he laughed in my face. He told me he'd been fanciful and dreamy in his youth but his grandfather, who had raised him on a big dairy farm, had beaten such nonsense out of him." She shook her head. "He was a lost cause. There was the son — John's grandson — but his father held me back. I was getting desperate. The Guardian Circle decided to wait until he grew older and then approach him on our own. After I came back to Canada, we heard that Richard and his wife had died in a plane crash. Her family didn't want the boy. They thought he was common." She smiled, a funny, twisted smile.

"Did you get to see him?" I asked.

"It took a while but I convinced the family that he would be better off in Canada, where one of their cousins had a small farm. The boy was terribly nervous and overly imaginative and they were glad to get rid of him. I arranged for the boy to come to Winnipeg. It was important to have him in the city where John had lived. He was a very sensitive child. Very gifted. But true to MacCaw form, he fought me all the way."

"Who was he? How — ?"

"Rachel!" laughed Will. "Wake up! The boy is your dad!"

Dad? John MacCaw's grandson? His paintings in all their swirling colours appeared in my mind. I should have realized. Maybe I hadn't wanted to admit it to myself. Because then, it meant that he'd known all along that I was different, too. And he hadn't explained things to me. Things that I had a right to know.

I stood in front of my aunt. "So how come he isn't the next in line? Why not Dad?"

I got my answer when the door behind us burst open and Alan MacCaw charged into the room.

Chapter 26

"What the hell is going on here?" he bellowed. "Irene! What's happening?"

We all stared at the tall slender man with the blazing eyes and dark red hair. He seemed like a stranger in his blue jeans, denim work shirt and red down-filled jacket. He brought with him the smell of cold air and diesel fumes. Max, who'd been snoring contentedly under Mr. Basely's chair, awoke with a loud snort and struggled from below to protect us. He sat down with a thump when I ran past.

"Dad!" I cried. "You did come!" I was going to throw my arms around him, but something about the way he looked at me made me stop.

He seemed confused, staring down at me, searching my face. "Are you okay? I thought — " He grabbed me in a big bear hug. His voice was choked. "I've called so many times." He held me at arm's length, his hands gripping my shoulders. "Why didn't you ever come to the phone? You sounded frantic last night. What's going on?"

"I didn't know you'd phoned. They . . . that is, Aunt Irene didn't tell me. Last night I could barely hear you. I wanted you to come home!"

He turned to Aunt Irene. "Irene! Damn you! You promised me! You said she wouldn't be involved in any of your hocus-pocus. You promised me you'd protect her — let her have a regular life — no hassles." His eyes narrowed. "I should have known better." He took a giant step towards her and shouted, "You promised!"

Aunt Irene retreated behind Mr. Basely's chair, as if the old man could somehow protect her from the anger that pulsed off Dad like a strobe light. "I . . . I didn't really promise that, Alan, my dear. I didn't *actually* promise. You know yourself, if you'd agreed to help years ago, before you were married, we wouldn't have had to . . ."

"To use a young girl?" demanded Dad. "She's just a kid, for god's sakes!"

Will stood up, his ear tips blazing. "If you were so worried, then why did you let Rachel come to stay here?" He saw the look on Dad's face and he slowly sank back down again. "Uh . . . just wondering . . . sir."

Dad shook his head. "Because I'm a fool, son. Because *she* promised me she was finished with all this . . . this business. She showed up one day when I was really desperate. I didn't know

202

what I was going to do to make sure Rachel was safe while I travelled."

"But you turned me away," Aunt Irene said, in a small voice.

Dad ran his hand over his face. "Yeah, and then like a fool I let you have Rachel." He looked at me and I saw a kind of desperation in his face. "When Joanna left, Irene just showed up. She told me she was only concerned about your well-being. I — I loved her for caring enough to watch over you until I found us a place to stay. Shows you how bloody psychic I am! I fell for it. I actually fell for it."

"I had to tell you a little white lie," said Aunt Irene. "It was — "

Dad pushed past me as if he might hit Aunt Irene. I grabbed his arm and held on. "Dad! Wait!"

I could feel him shaking from head to toe. "What were you going to do with her?" he snarled. "Eh? Sacrifice her to some demon god? To those faces I see in my dreams? It's sick. Twisted and sick!"

"Dad! Please!" I cried. "You don't understand!"

"Get your things, Rachel. We're getting out of here."

"But, Dad. Did you have Warnings, too? When you were a kid, did you have them like I do?"

For the first time, he hesitated. He looked at me, shaking his head as if clearing it. "What? Rachel, what are you talking about? Have they messed around in your mind with all this garbage?"

"Dad. Did you — did you know things before they happened? Did you hear things that weren't there? Smell things that weren't there? See things that weren't there? Things that came true a few hours or even days later?"

"Rachel." Dad's face was set. "Get your things. We're leaving."

"Did you, Dad? Did you? Just answer me. Did you?"

Dad looked around at the small group of frightened old people, at the long-legged, red-eared boy and then at me staring solemnly up at him.

"What difference does it make, Rachel? This woman," he pointed at Aunt Irene, "is as batty as hell. So are her friends. They've brainwashed you. Into their stupid way of thinking. Something I've been fighting all my life."

"All your life? Since you were a kid?" I asked. "Like me, then."

His dark eyes narrowed and I knew he was seeing the pictures of past times flashing through his mind. Taking his hand, I pulled him into the room. Like a sleep-walker he followed. Slumping into an empty chair, he scrubbed his hands over his face and through his hair.

"I prayed this would never happen, Rachel." A muscle beside his eye was twitching. He reached out and grabbed my hand and held it between his own. "It's my fault you're in this mess. I shouldn't have trusted her. I knew she'd

let me down . . . when last night, last night — "
His voice broke.

"What happened last night, Dad?"

"I was driving from Brandon to Regina. And suddenly I saw you. You were standing in a dark shadow and it was closing over you, sucking you into it — away from me. I turned the truck around. But it started to snow — sleet and rain mixed — and then the truck broke down. That's when I called you. It took me forever to fix the damn thing."

"So you get Warnings. Like me," I said.

His long face was open and sad and for just a second he reminded me of John. "Yes," he said, finally. "I get them. I was ten when I came to live with my cousin here in Manitoba. He and his wife were good people. When I started having these — these strange things happen again — I knew I couldn't tell them. I was either crazy or a freak. Then Aunt Irene came to the farm. She told me I was special. I liked her very much, but I thought she was nutty, too. I decided that if I didn't listen to her, I would be okay."

"I know how you felt," I muttered.

He looked at me sharply. "I had to stay in control of my feelings and thoughts all the time. Even when I was in art school and the others smoked dope and drank, I couldn't. I had to stay in control. I could draw and paint a better world. But when I married Joanna, and you were born, the dreams got worse and I became frightened for you. Maybe the insanity was inherited."

"But what you were dreaming was real," I said.

He shook his head. "I couldn't believe that. Yet I'd started painting images that frightened me, that seemed to come from inside me. I knew I had to protect you. I moved us to a farm. I gave up painting. Work hard, don't think — that became my life."

"And you left Joanna out?" I asked.

He nodded. "She wouldn't have understood."

"You didn't give her a chance to."

He looked at me hard. "She wouldn't have understood."

I nodded. "You're probably right. And when I tried to tell you about the fire alarm at school and about Spark, you knew I had it, too, didn't you?"

He nodded. "I figured if I didn't let on, you would learn to suppress them. Like I did."

"Dad. That shadow you saw around me. It's real. It's found us. It's after me. We have to fight it!"

He stood up. "No. We'll get you away. I can't allow you to be a part of this. We'll find a good hiding place."

"But, Dad, that's what John did. He didn't believe his mother, Bethia. And Grandfather Richard didn't believe Aunt Irene. They spent their whole lives hiding their real selves. And probably worrying, just like you. We can't be like Bethia or John."

"Bethia. Who's that? And who is this John?"

I sat down on the floor and told Dad the story of Bethia and John and Dunstan Gregor. And I told him about the Stone and the dangers of giving it to the black cold shadow. I explained that John was getting weak. Losing his hold on the secret of where the Stone was. And that the shadow would never leave me alone. Not unless we fought back. Not unless we helped John MacCaw and the Guardian Circle. And for that, he'd have to stay right here.

Chapter 27

When I was finished, I looked at my father. He remained sitting without moving, staring at his callused hands.

"Dad?" I whispered, moving close. "I need your help. The Fossils . . . I mean, the Guardians are worried that they won't be able to do it on their own. I can't leave them."

He looked at me and his eyes were shadowed. "We'd be better off on our own. Let them sort out their own problems."

I looked at Aunt Irene. "Can't you tell him how much I need him?"

"Alan, dear," said Aunt Irene, "we've told you everything. It's urgent. John needs our help. Tonight."

Dad rubbed his hands up and down his face and through his hair. "I'm so tired, I can't see straight. I can't think." He looked around at the

Fossils. "You're asking too much of her. And of me." He leaned forward. "You could be over-reacting to a danger that simply doesn't exist."

I sat back amazed. "Dad! How can you say that. Don't you believe us?"

Dad stood up and I scrambled to my feet. He looked down at me. "I'm going to lie down, if there's a place for me. Then I'm going to have a shower and change. Then we're all going to talk about this sensibly. I think we all need time to calm down."

Aunt Irene put a hand lightly on his arm. "You know what your duty is, Alan. You've been avoiding it for many years. Now we need you. You're a Gregor. You can't let a child, your own daughter, take on this responsibility. But she will, if you won't. Will you think seriously about that?"

"Rachel *is* my first concern, Irene," Dad said. "I don't like this. I don't like any of it. Don't count on us staying. I can easily take her away. You know that." He looked at her steadily and she nodded grimly.

Gladys rushed forward. "Never mind that now. You need to rest. I'll show you to your room. You must rest up. Luther can sit with you while I prepare a special meal, a very VERY special supper for you — something light but nutritious." She patted Dad's back. "We've had your room ready for ages, haven't we, Irenie?" *Bat, bat, bat*, went the dusty eyelashes.

Irene nodded sadly. "Yes. We knew you would come. With Rachel here. It was only a matter of time. I'm sorry it had to be this way."

That's when it hit me. Hard in the chest. I'd been used. I stood staring stiffly at my father, seeing him as the others must. Not as my father, but as Alan MacCaw, Protector of the Stone. It was him they'd wanted all along.

He ran his hand through his coppery hair. "You've been clever, Aunt Irene. But it's like I said. She's all I have."

"Then you'll have to think about protecting her," she answered, quietly. "Will you at least think about that?"

Dad stood stiff and his voice was cold. "I'll decide what I think is best. But yes, I'll think about it."

"Good lad," said Mr. Basely.

"Can't ask for more than that," said a subdued Luther.

Mitzi leaned towards me. "What is it, kiddo? Are you worried about your dad?"

My cheeks were burning and my pulse was beating sickeningly in my throat. "So! You said you were saving the room for someone. You made it sound as if you were waiting for another old person. Someone I didn't know. But it was Dad all along, wasn't it? You knew he would come, didn't you? You horrible old fakes!"

Aunt Irene looked helplessly at the other Fossils. Will put his hand on my shoulder, but I pushed if off and shouted at him, "See, Will? They knew he would come. Because they had me! As bait!" I turned to the old people. "You used me. To trap my dad. You let me think I was the centre of everything. But I wasn't, was

I? That's why we had to wait. That's why you wouldn't tell me anything! That's why you kept me from talking to him on the phone. So that he'd get worried and come. Today, when you figured he wasn't coming, you knew you'd be stuck with second best. Me!" My eyes filled with scalding tears. "You're no different than my mother. You don't care about anything but yourselves. And . . . and you've just used me again. Right now! You got me so convinced about everything that I begged him to stay. Which is exactly what you wanted. I . . . I thought you needed me to help you. Me! But you didn't. You don't care about me. Not one bit. You want him! And even now, when he says he'll think about it, you can hardly keep from jumping up and down and cheering! Well, I hope he does decide to walk right out of here, because I intend to!"

The Fossils rushed forward and clustered around me. No, no, no, they cried, it wasn't like that at all. Mr. Basely, his blanket around his shoulders, leaned into the circle and touched my flaming cheek with his cool fingertips. I twisted away. I didn't want any of them near me.

Through a kind of dark curtain I saw my father standing there. For a moment I felt myself fill up with hatred for him. *I* was supposed to be the one. And he arrives and they practically slobber all over him. And he doesn't even want to help. I heard a faint chuckle somewhere in the room. I felt myself straighten up to stare them all down.

"Rachel? Honey, hold on," said Dad. "Look,

we'll talk it over. You and me. We can leave if you want. Believe me, I didn't know what they were up to."

"But you let her take me, didn't you," I said in a low voice. "You knew deep down that she would use me."

"I didn't, I — " he began.

"Rachel, my dear. We've been through so much together. Please," said Mr. Basely. "Try to understand. We had no way of knowing how to handle this. We knew we had a deadline, we just didn't know when it would be. We knew that your father was the stonger choice, but we also knew he might have lost some of his gifts from battling against them. And so we needed you. We still do."

"Yeah, kiddo, that's right. And hey, we've loved having you here," offered Mitzi, searching for a Kleenex up her sleeve and handing it to me. I ignored it and wiped my face with the palms of my hands. "We never realized how much fun having a kid around could be. Then we started to worry about you, see? *Really* worry about you. So, we started thinking about the risk — to you. Before that, we didn't think we'd get to care so much about you."

Will piped up. "Gee, Rachel, you gotta see their point. You're just a kid and — "

"And if my dad stays and does his brilliant job of getting this stupid stone, then I'm finished. Out I'd go, right?" I turned on Will. "And just what is their point? They take what they want and to heck with anyone else, right? That's their point!"

Luther took my chin in his long fingers and tilted my head up. I refused to look at him. "You don't believe that, Rachel. Your home is here as long as you want it to be. You know that. You'd learn along with your father. And someday you'll take over from him. Even now, if he does decide against us, I believe you'd stay and fight, no matter what. Wouldn't you?"

"No, I wouldn't!" I said angrily, pulling my chin from his grip.

"You're young, kiddo," said Mitzi. "You should be able to enjoy your young years without the weight of this trouble. That's why, when we got to know you, we hoped . . . your dad . . . you know . . . would come."

"Come on, Rach . . . We were both pretty scared . . ." Will began. "And now with your dad here — "

"Oh shut up, Will. Just shut up! A lot of help you are. I should have known you wouldn't go through to the finish. Just like everyone else. Why don't you take off? Now! Everyone else does. Everyone! Isn't that right, Dad? Well, I'm leaving! And I'm not ever staying with any of you again!"

I turned, but stopped dead when I saw what hung in silent darkness across the open doorway. Waiting. For me. In my distant ear, I heard a sort of gurgling chuckle. In the next moment it had changed to a subdued, soothing hum. Then, it was calling my name, over and over. The shadow swirled and moved back into the hallway, its black wings rustling. I felt a swell of sympathy and warmth wash over me, pulling me towards it. I took a step forward.

"Come," a distant voice said. "I'll take care of you. That's right. Come closer."

Someone gripped my shoulder from behind.

"Rachel? What is it?" asked Aunt Irene.

"Yes, yes, what is it?" muttered the Fossils, peering through the door.

Will stood next to me. "It's there, isn't it?"

I nodded.

"Dunstan thinks there's a chance you're not going to help us. He thinks you're the most vulnerable," said Mr. Basely, softly, coming so close I could feel his breath on the back of my neck. "He and his group think you will come to them. Rachel, listen to me. You've misunderstood us. Your father will add great strength to this fight. But he is new to it. No different than you. We need both of you. Together. We won't let you go."

The single voice from the shadow calling my name changed into many voices, pleading, softly begging me. It was me and only me they wanted.

Mr. Basely's voice became more urgent. "We need you, Rachel. Your father needs you. We love you, Rachel. Your father came, not because of us, but because he loves you — because he wanted to protect you, because he needed you!"

The shadow drew nearer, pulling at me, calling me. Slowly the Fossils surrounded Will and me. I didn't know what to do. I looked at them — Luther, Mitzi, Aunt Irene, Mr. Basely. And then at my father. He took my hand and squeezed it so hard, I felt my bones fold over each other. The Fossils closed around Will and

Dad and me. The shadow grew, darkening the hall. Dad's head jerked up.

"My god, is that him?" whispered Dad. "Is that — "

I nodded.

I felt myself pulled into the circle of his arm. His other one went around Will.

"Get away," he snarled at the shadow. "You won't get her. Get away." He was shaking, but his voice was deep, furious. "Rachel, tell it to go away."

I hesitated. The shadow drifted to the door opening. Dad stepped in front of me, turning his back on the shadow. All I saw was his jean shirt and red jacket. The zipper was broken. I looked up. A vein in his neck was pounding. His eyes were open wide, the bridge of his nose and cheekbones white as if the skin had stretched tight.

"Rachel," he said, "I love you. Don't . . . don't fight me. We'll work together on this. I know I've screwed up. But let me fix it. Let me try. Please, Rachel."

"Rach?" said Will. I looked at him. "It's okay. Honest. We'll work it out."

"Oh, I . . . don't . . ." I blinked back more tears. "I thought . . ." I felt swamped. I broke away from my dad and ran to the lavendar warmth of Aunt Irene's chest.

"Never mind, never mind," she murmured. "It's all our fault. We didn't make things clear. Oh, Rachel."

When I dared to look again the shadow was gone. I heaved a deep sigh and leaned against her. She stroked my hair again and again.

"My god! If people could botch up anything more, I bet we could do it," said Mitzi. "Heaven only knows what more will happen."

Dad stood alone in the middle of the room. In a hollow voice, he said, "How much time do you have?"

"It will have to be tonight," said Aunt Irene. "You and Rachel know everything now. You are at risk all the time, as you just saw. You are both very vulnerable."

"Rachel? Is this what you want? Believe me I — " Dad started.

I moved close to Will and looked down at my feet. I knew I should go up to Dad and hug him and tell him it was all right, but I just couldn't.

"What should I do?" I heard Dad say. "Rachel, tell me, I — "

Mitzi spoke sharply to Dad. "Listen, *you* have to decide. Now, you know what we're up against. I'm not one to pussyfoot around even if others are. Either you're in or you're out. Enough is enough."

Dad nodded. "All right. For Rachel's protection, I'm in." He took a step towards me. "Rachel? Honey, I — "

"Give the girl some time alone," said Luther. "She's been through a lot. Thanks to us. Some Guardian Circle we are. You're tired, Alan. We'll take you to your room, Mitzi and me, and let Rachel sort herself out. Okay, Rachel?"

I nodded, not looking at my father. Dad allowed himself to be led out of the room by Mitzi and Luther. Gladys followed behind mumbling

216

something about a spinach soufflé. As they turned into the hallway, Dad stopped. I looked up. He smiled sadly and raised one hand, just as when he'd driven away in his big truck. I looked down again. The door closed behind them.

Chapter 28

"We had no choice, Rachel," said Mr. Basely. "But if you search your feelings you'll know how deeply we care about you. You do know that, don't you?"

I shrugged, and took the hanky Aunt Irene held out to me.

"And you know I'm not going anywhere, eh?" said Will lightly.

I hiccupped.

"Are you willing to work with us tonight, dear girl?" asked Mr. Basely gently.

"Yes," I whispered. "But Will has to be here, too. If he wants to come, that is."

Will grinned and I knew he'd accepted my apology. "Hey, I wouldn't miss this for anything."

"I don't know — " said Mr. Basely, shaking his head.

"I promise to do everything you ask me," Will pleaded. "I won't be a bother at all. I'll keep my mouth shut. Anything. Just let me be here. Please?"

Mr. Basely looked at Aunt Irene. "What about his parents?" she said. "We've met *Mrs.* Lennox, don't forget. Oh — I'm sorry, Will."

"He has to come!" I cried. "I won't do it without him."

Mr. Basely nodded. "Irene?"

"As long as it doesn't come back on us later. I must say, he's stood by Rachel through it all," she said.

Will looked excited and terrified at the same time. I felt the same way. I walked over to him and grabbed his hand. Hard. He flinched.

"For now, I want Will to go home and think this over very seriously," said Aunt Irene. "Rachel and I will make tea and biscuits for everyone. If you decide to come back, Will, be here at eight o'clock sharp."

"Right," said Will.

Aunt Irene nodded, touched his arm lightly. "See him to the door, dear. Quentin, you lie down until dinner. Rachel, come into the kitchen as soon as you've said goodbye." She left the room, taking Mr. Basely with her.

I walked Will to the front door.

"This is it, huh?" he said, resting his arms on either side of my neck and looking down at me.

I leaned forward until my forehead rested against the sweater between his open jacket. I could feel his unsteady heartbeats pulse through my head. They matched my own.

"Try to see your dad's side of things, eh?" he said. "He really cares about you."

"I'll try," I murmured. "I thought I was the only one who could save things. What an ego, huh?"

"Yeah. What an ego," he said.

I punched his arm. "I hope things go right for us," I said softly.

"Do you mean tonight? Or do you mean us — you and me?" he asked smiling. "This is me trying for light comic relief."

I smiled. "See you at eight. Okay?" I tried not to make it sound like I was pleading.

"Wouldn't miss this for the other-world," he said, lightly. He lowered his head and touched his lips to mine. "I'll be here." He pulled the door open and in a swirl of frosted air, he was gone.

Chapter 29

On the dot of eight I led him upstairs.

"Everything's ready," I whispered. "Good thing you missed dinner. Gladys really outdid herself. A spinach soufflé like a giant spongy football. Green! Ugh. You should have seen Dad's face." I giggled.

"Poor guy," said Will. "How's he doing otherwise?"

I felt a prickle of irritability but fought it off. *"He's* doing fine. Gladys has fallen for him in a big way." I fluttered my eyelashes at him and simpered.

Will put out his hand. "And you?"

"Ah, I'm okay. Aunt Irene and I talked for quite a while. I see their point. But they *did* use me. She admits it. They weren't sure if Dad would make it in time and then I'd have been the only one. And she's right — with the two of us, we probably stand a better chance. It'll take some getting used to, having him around. Of course she's as pleased as punch. Mr. Basely looks pretty tired, but Luther's just given him a dose of something purple and sticky, so he'll be okay. Mitzi got one look at Gladys's monster soufflé and told us she's going to cook every second day. At least one good thing came out of today." I was talking too much and too fast, but I couldn't help myself.

Half-way up the stairs, Will stopped. "So? Is your dad going through with it?" I looked down at him. He leaned up and caught my chin with a soft warm kiss.

"After he had his rest and a shower, he met with Mr. Basely. For hours. Aunt Irene was there, too. Then he came and told me again that he was really sorry. I think I know what he's gone through all his life. I've been there myself. But I'm having trouble figuring out why he did things the way he did. He should have told me sooner. Especially when I tried to talk to him about it last summer. He said he hardly understood the Warnings himself. So how could he help me? He said he'd known for years he'd have to come to terms with his handicap sometime. He calls it his *handicap*."

"Isn't that what you thought it was?"

"I guess I did."

"So he's not going to grab you and run?"

At the top of the stairs, I took his hand. "No. He won't run. He's really excited. I saw it in his face."

We shook our heads at Dad's complete turn-about. When we reached the bottom of the attic stairs, we stood side by side and stared up.

"Have you seen the set-up?" he asked in a low voice.

"They wouldn't let me. They've been dragging furniture around for hours, and running up and down stairs collecting stuff. Will? I'm nervous."

"We're only going to try and arm wrestle with the shadow of Dunstan Gregor who died a hundred years ago. What's there to be nervous of?"

We looked at each other with wide eyes.

"Not very funny, am I?" he asked.

"Even joking, it sounds so awful, doesn't it?" I whispered. "It's a lot different than talking to John. That was almost nice, but the shadow is . . . well, it's . . ."

"I know. But at least everyone will be there to help. Ready?"

I gulped air. "I guess so."

The stairs creaked under our feet. When we rounded the corner, a soft yellow light lit the last few treads. The two old chairs had been pushed against the wall with the rolled-up rug. In the centre of the floor stood a large round wooden table. Eight of the dining-room chairs had been placed around it. White candles in single candlesticks had been placed around the room, some on the desk, others on the floor, and one large one on a stand not far from the table. All the chairs except two were occupied.

"Come in, my dears," said Aunt Irene, with

a sweep of her arm. She looked tall and beautiful, wearing a loose silky gown with full sleeves and wide combs in her hair.

Everyone had dressed up except for Will and me. Even Dad had put on a clean white shirt and flannel trousers. His hair, freshly washed, shone smooth in the candlelight. I pulled at the waist of my jeans, and made sure my T-shirt was tucked in.

I suddenly felt very shy. Dad's long face, narrow arched nose and hooded eyes gave him an air like a prince. He didn't look anything like the dusty farmer I'd known most of my life. This must have been the man that Joanna had fallen in love with. For the first time ever, I sympathized with my mother. It must have been awful to watch him change over the years.

When he lifted his gaze and looked at me, I saw in his eyes something new and strange and intense. For a second I thought he didn't know me. Then his face softened slightly and he smiled. "Come on, honey. Sit down across from me. Mr. Basely is going to tell us what to do."

"Wh-what about me?" Will asked, gripping my hand tightly.

"Sit over there, kiddo," said Mitzi, pointing to the empty chair between Dad and Irene. "Keep your eyes open and your mouth closed. Think you can do both?"

Will nodded, let go of my hand and crept to his chair, looking left and right. I think he was scouting for strange shadows that might be sliding along the walls outside of the circle of light. Finally, he sat down and gave me a weak smile.

When I sat down, Mr. Basely cleared his throat. "In a moment, we will make a chain of hands around the circle. As I told you at supper, this creates a ring of energy for John to lock into. I should warn you that strange things may happen. The important thing is not, under any circumstances, to break the Guardian Circle. We are inviting John to join us, but we don't want an opening for Dunstan Gregor."

I heard a distant snigger of laughter and caught the movement of a dark shape along the far wall. I sat forward. "He's already here. I can feel him. Dad, can you?"

Dad nodded once sharply, his eyes sombre.

Mr. Basely spoke quickly, his eyes darting left and right. "Dunstan will try very hard to get in. We must not break the safety of the circle."

"Right," said Dad. "I'm ready. Rachel?"

I wasn't, but I nodded anyway. Across the table, Dad grinned, as if to say, "Isn't this exciting? Isn't this amazing?" I knew he was trying to be reassuring, but it didn't help. The muscles in my legs just wouldn't stop shaking. If I'd had to stand up, I'm sure I would have fallen over.

Will looked like he was about to take off on a bucking bronco — no hands. He looked so funny, I wanted to laugh hysterically and had to swallow down the urge in big gulps.

Mr. Basely held one finger in the air. "Ready? Wait . . . wait . . . now!"

I took Luther's hand on one side and Mitzi's on the other. As soon as the last hand was gripped, tremors began deep in the basement of the house, tremors that echoed and resounded with vast rumblings and clattering of doors as they travelled up.

I held my breath as the attic began to vibrate. Down below we could hear tables, chairs, cabinets and desks throughout the house shifting with loud scrapings and crashes. Glass shattered. I could almost see the paintings in the hallways swinging on their wires as a strong wind blew through the house, along the halls, spiralling up the staircase. It burst into the room like air out of a monstrous balloon — with a loud screech followed by a huge trembling sigh. Debris clattered or fluttered to the floor — papers, china, books, Aunt Irene's fur hat and one red mitt. Mine. And then . . . sudden silence.

Dad was sitting straight up in his chair and on his face was a look of astonishment and immense excitement. The battle had begun.

Chapter 30

The deadly silence continued. I caught Aunt Irene's eye and we smiled tremulously at each other, like shipmates about to take an unknown voyage.

Gladys's eyes were shut. Her bottom lip quivered, a few small squeaks escaping now and again. Luther, his skull head shadowed, peered with hollow eyes around the room, alert for any sound. Mitzi, sucking on a large peppermint, stared defiantly ahead, looking as if she'd like to tackle Dunstan Gregor single-handedly. Mr. Basely looked as if he was presiding over a Board meeting, his white bandage the only sign that anything was wrong. Will's eyes were travelling all around the room, his big ears almost wavering with anxiety. The stranger, Alan MacCaw, sat very still, waiting, his eyes shining.

I didn't notice the faint ball of light until it

moved behind Dad's head. The light grew stronger until it seemed to shine right through his skull, finally enveloping his head like a gossamer scarf.

Dad began to speak, but not with his own voice. John's face, like a fine veil, had formed in front of his.

"We must move quickly," the voice said, "as my uncle is assembling. I must pass on the Stone before he is completed for presentation to this world. I will place it on the table in the centre of the Guardian Circle. But you must concentrate on holding it there or you could lose it. I can't hold onto the Stone without your help. Not with my dear uncle skulking around."

Everyone waited. The gossamer face closed its eyes. Dad's eyes closed as well.

"Look," cried Gladys. "Over there. The storeroom door! There!" I looked over my shoulder fearfully, expecting to see the door slowly opening. What I actually saw was a small bright light where the glass doorknob had been.

"So that's where you hid it!" I cried. "It was right in view all along! Disguised as the doorknob!"

"Look!" gasped Will. "It's . . . it's coming right out of the door! It's . . . it's coming . . . towards . . ."

"Us!" breathed Gladys, helpfully. "Ooo! Ooo! Here it comes!"

The Stone flew across the room, whirled above our heads and then it lowered itself onto the tabletop. In the candle-light it seemed to pulsate, to breathe. It grew bigger and began to change shape. It was clear, like crystal water, and shaped like an egg cut in half from tip to tip. As it turned slowly on its narrower tip, I saw that the flat side was carved with animals, no, flowers, no . . . stars — each time it turned it changed its carvings.

"Well, I'll be . . ." said Luther. "Well done, well done."

"Thank you," said John. He stood beside Dad's left shoulder — a slender young man in a brown dressing-gown. He looked like Dad's son, not his grandfather. "Here I am . . . not exactly in the flesh, as it were, but here all the same. Thanks to all of you. I must quickly pass control of the Stone to you, Alan. My grandson. Curious, isn't it?" His hand rested briefly on Dad's shoulder. Dad looked up at him and they smiled.

He then turned his gaze on me. "Hi," I said in a small voice, realizing too late how stupid I sounded.

"My dear, dear girl," was all he said, but I felt as if a gentle hand had touched me. He looked around the Circle of Gregor. "I fear we have a fight on our hands, my friends. Short and vigorous. Am I right, Uncle?" He addressed the last sentence to the darkness at our backs.

A current of icy air skimmed over our hands. It passed by again, higher this time, chilling our faces. A rumbling noise echoed through the attic, growing louder and louder until it burst into deep reverberating chuckles. I felt the hair on my head shiver over my scalp.

"Don't break the circle," called John over the

noise. "Hang on, my friends." He placed both hands on Dad's shoulders.

The wind grew colder and stronger, making my face ache. It tore at everyone's hair, making our eyes flutter against the onslaught. We didn't move our hands. The wind died down to a hissing whisper.

"Wh-what should we be doing?" asked Aunt Irene.

"We have to confront Dunstan Gregor," said Dad.

John nodded agreement, his pale face worried. "I have little fight left. You will have to do most of it. He thinks he can wear you down with parlour tricks and fear — make you break the circle so he can grab the Stone. But we must use the Stone to bring him to the circle. You must turn it three times, Alan. By using your mind. You can do it. Rachel can help. The Stone will stop when it's facing him and he will have to show himself." He pointed to the Gregor Stone. "Now!"

Slowly the little Stone began to turn.

"That's it. Remember," he said, "don't break the ring of hands or he will be able to reach in and get it. That's right. Concentrate, Alan. Good. Rachel? Good!"

The Stone turned three times and when it stopped, its flat side, clear and unblemished, faced me. I held my breath. John leaned closer to Dad and spoke. Dad nodded.

"Well, Dunstan Gregor, let's see you!" Dad said in a determined voice.

I stared straight ahead, preparing myself for

the terrible darkness of the shadow. Instead, with a loud *reoow*, a huge orange cat landed on the table. Except for one or two loud gasps, no one spoke. The cat blinked slowly in the candle-light and began to pace with padded feet across the linked hands of the circle.

"Good god!" spluttered Mitzi. "Where did this bloody cat come from? Whose is it?"

Gladys, looking as if she might swoon away, whispered with eyes tightly shut, "It's that big tom-cat I told you about, Rachel, I'd know it anywhere."

The cat slunk up to her and stared until she opened one eye. She closed it quickly with a gargled moan.

"Don't be scared, Gladys," I said. "It's only Roger."

The cat turned and stared at me, its yellow eyes like flat gold coins in the candle-light. The Stone rolled until its open end faced him. In an instant, the cat became Roger, a tiny Roger, small and spitting mad. He stood up on his bare feet and ran towards me, hissing and snarling. Max, with thumps and scrabbling nails, launched himself from under the table. Once out in the open, he crouched, his big muscles bunched for an attack, his sightless eyes burning with an intense light.

"No, Max!" I cried.

"Wait!" shouted Dad and John together. "The Stone will make him go!" cried John. "He will go! Go!"

Roger swung around and launched himself at John. But before he reached that side of the table, he disappeared, leaving behind a faint mournful mew.

"Good grief," said Luther, "I've heard of people who look like their pets, but never one who *was* his own pet."

"Luther," gasped Aunt Irene, "how can you make jokes at a time like this?"

"Would you rather I ran around the room screaming myself silly?" he retorted. "And break the chain?"

"Stop it at once," demanded Mr. Basely. "Look at Rachel!"

I stiffened. "What?"

"There's a huge . . . *thing* right behind you," shouted Will. "Somebody. Do something!"

I could smell the shadow's heavy stench float over me.

"So, here we are, Uncle," said John, in a faint, hollow voice. He took a deep breath. "It's all right, Rachel. The Stone has him. He will have to show himself now. He won't dupe us this time."

Out of the corner of my eye, I saw the shadow float with fluid grace from the searching side of the Stone, stopping behind Will's chair. Poor Will sat bolt upright, his eyes swivelling back and forth trying to glimpse the creature without turning his head.

"It . . . is . . . he . . . there?" he babbled. "I mean . . . has he gone . . . is he there?"

"It's okay, son," said Dad. "The Stone has him."

He was right. The Stone was keeping in line with the shadow's movements, which had stopped between Gladys and Dad. Larger and thicker and blacker it grew, until, like a zipper opening on a giant cape, it slowly split to reveal the figure of my great-great uncle, Dunstan Gregor.

Chapter 31

This couldn't be Dunstan Gregor, the evil-smelling shadow that had tried to suffocate me. I stared, my mouth open in amazement.

The shadow remained around the figure like the hooded curve of a cobra. Inside it stood a tall thin man. His suit of clothes were old-fashioned but very elegant with white collar and cuffs. His hair was thick and parted in the middle, showing off a high, smooth forehead and wide-spaced eyes under winged brows. Under the long straight nose was a delicately pointed moustache. His chin was firm and his mouth wide. His amused gaze took in the huddled group around the table.

"Well, well, well. So here we are. The clan survives. All the ingredients for a rather shaky but, I have to confess, complete Guardian Circle — the four descendants of my dear mother, a loyal band of followers, and best of all — " his eyes fell upon the Stone " — and best of all, my lovely little Stone. I must say, Nephew, you've hidden youself very well. I've had quite a time finding you."

His voice was deep and smooth and mesmerizing.

"Yes," he continued, "with my little Stone and with little Rachel here, and Alan if he chooses to join my merry band, I should have quite a bit of fun and adventure. We could really stir up some excitement all around, I'd say. Alan here has quite an understanding of me and my little group. But I think you were a little harsh on us, my dear fellow." He reached forward, opened his hand and, from nowhere, Dad's paintings fell on the table and slowly unrolled. The pale beautiful one with the smiling faces had been sliced through and through, but the other two glistened in the candle-light. I gasped. "Yes, I took them, Rachel. We, on this side, have respect for your father's talents. He could continue if he joined us. Provided we don't have any sentimental slop like that pasty-faced one. Made me positively ill. So gooey sweet. Revolting." The paintings disappeared.

Dad stared at Dunstan Gregor, his hooded lids lowered, his eyes glittering in the slits. Dunstan's satisfied smile staggered off his face and he turned away from Dad's steady gaze and fastened on John.

"Aah, Nephew," said Dunstan, his smile returning. "Aaah, now, even if Alan refuses, you could join us. What fun! We could control a great

deal of power if we used Rachel on this side."
He stepped closer and leaned over Gladys's
shoulder. She whimpered and closed her eyes.
"Think of it, Nephew. Think of the power. The
control."

John swayed and I saw his hands grip Dad.
He seemed to lurch to one side. In slow motion,
I saw Dad's hand reach up and cover one of
John's.

"Dad!" I screeched. "Don't! The circle!"

But he was too late. Dunstan had already
stepped out of the shadow and reached into the
centre of the table to snatch the Stone.

"Put it down, Dunstan."

Who'd said that? All of us, Dunstan included,
looked around.

"Put it down, Dunstan," said the voice again.
"You cannot have it. It was mine to give to
whom I wished. And I gave it to John."

"Bethia! Damn you!" cried Dunstan Gregor.
He didn't release the Stone, but remained leaning over the table.

A small figure moved out of the shadows and
stopped beside John. It was a dumpy little
woman with a swirling knot of reddish grey hair.
She wore a long plain dress. "We've had a time
finding you, John. You hid well. Too well. We'd
almost given up hope." Almost casually, she
reached over and covered Dunstan Gregor's
hand with her own. "So, we kept an eye on you
instead, Dunstan. We knew you'd find him
eventually."

"Bethia! It's not fair," cried Dunstan, "you

can't come here. It's my battle. My battle with the false protector of the Stone. The Stone isn't yours any more." He stamped his feet and the floor shook.

The woman smiled sweetly. "That's where you're wrong, brother dear. You never did take the time to learn the ways. It will always be mine. The rightful protectors never give up their claim on the Stone. We pass it on. But it is still ours."

Dunstan poked his chest with the fingers of his free hand and a heavy cloud of dust rose from the fabric. "But I am the rightful owner. I was next in line. Not you. Mother had no right! No right at all! It's mine. Let go of my hand. Let go, let go!" he screeched.

"Listen to yourself, Dunstan," said Bethia, in a soothing calm voice. "You haven't changed a bit. A greedy, selfish brat. You were always a spoiled, cruel bully. Now, it's my turn to bully you. I don't have much time, but I've been allowed to make sure you don't get this Stone."

She lifted her brother's fingers one by one away from the stone. With a scream of rage, he backed away, staring at his hand as if it had been burned. His cool elegance was completely gone, and in its place I saw a face tortured and bloated with fury. He paced back and forth behind Gladys, hands clenched at his side.

"It's not right. It's not fair. Bethia, you have no right. I hate you. You have no right. *No right!* It's mine. I'll get it. Somehow, I will. Yes, I will." He came to a stop and lifted his hands, fists clenched. Then he looked out from between his raised arms. Straight at me.

In a swirl of blackness, he swept around the table and threw his shadowy cloak around me. I felt its familiar coolness close down over my head.

"I'll take her with me," he cried. "I'll keep her until you give me what's rightfully mine. She knows what it's like to be alone, with no one to care. *I'll* care for her. You all used her. Look at them, Rachel. Look at your father. Look how your so-called Guardian Circle watched over you. How smug they all are. No one really cares about you. You know that deep inside, don't you?"

My voice came very faint from my throat. "No. No," I said.

"Oh, but you do. They promised that you would be so important and then they celebrated your father's return. They don't care about you."

I shook my head. He was saying everything I'd been feeling. But they were my family. Mr. Basely had said how much they cared. The shadow tightened around me. I felt the anger rising. Maybe they'd all been lying. Maybe they were all like Joanna. A wave of utter hopelessness filled me. I felt myself lifted from the chair. I was falling. Down, down I tumbled into a deep well. When I drifted to a stop, I was standing in almost total darkness.

"Rachel."

I turned. Dunstan Gregor stood behind me, a strange reddish light around him. Behind him huddled a small group of long, drab people. "I have you now," he said, smiling, pleased with himself. "You know that I'll care for you. You'll get the Stone for me, won't you?"

"I won't stay," I cried. "You can't make me!"

He laughed. "Try and find a way out, child. As long as you have all this anger towards the Circle, you're easy enough to control. All I need is the Stone. I'm sure my colleagues would like to welcome you."

"Welcome, welcome," the others whispered. A soft murmuring chant filled my head as they floated forward, grey and dreadful. Their lips barely moved and their eyes seemed frozen from within. The voices came from far away — from an older time. Like skaters on black ice, they drifted past me, some circling behind, others to either side. The movement stopped and I saw many of them looking up. A sigh rustled through the still figures. I looked up, too.

A fine thread of light was coiling in a circle above us, and in the centre, I saw three small figures. John. And Bethia. And . . . and Dad! They smiled down at me and reached out their hands. I bent my knees, pushed myself into the air and kicked my legs. Like a swimmer under water, I floated slowly upwards. The bleak figures swarmed towards me, stretching out their long grey arms and plucking at my clothes. "Stay, stay," they cried, their voices rustling like dry leaves.

"Look out, you fools! Let me through," cried Dunstan pushing his way through the small crowd. He shook his fist at the circle. "You can't take her. Not until you give me the Stone! You can't. I won't let you."

Frantically I kicked away from his reaching hand. I floated up, up, towards the ring of light. Down below, I heard an awful cry and saw a shattering of wings that flapped and gathered and moved towards me. I kept my eyes on the circle of light. More figures began to form in the ring. There was Luther's head, smiling and nodding. And there was Aunt Irene. And Mitzi and Gladys and Mr. Basely. And Will! He was staring around as if lost. When he looked down and saw me, he waved madly and I stretched up to him. Behind them, I saw a long line of others — faint glowing figures winding along a trail of light inside the ring. The Gregor Clan, stretching back in time.

From the depths below me came a loud cry. I looked down and saw the layers of black wings grow smaller and smaller. But still the voice persisted. "I'll get it. I won't stop. I won't — "

I gave a few final hard kicks and moved up, up, up, away from the darkness.

"Rachel. Rachel, open your eyes now. It's over."

I heard Bethia's voice close to my ear. I opened my eyes to find the warm familiar faces of the circle looking across the table at me.

Dad knocked back his chair, rushed around the table and gathered me into his arms. "We did it," he whispered, "we did it."

Bethia turned to John. "Time has run out. Are you ready?" she asked softly.

"I don't know," said John. "They need to learn

how to use the Stone. So they won't have to hide away. So they can live a more open life. You heard him, Mother. He'll be back."

Bethia smiled. "Not for some time. He's more weakened than even he realizes. The Stone will help them. And they have their protective circle," she nodded at the Fossils, "their Guardian Circle. It did a good job."

The Fossils still looked pretty frazzled, but pleased at her praise.

With that she took John's hand and together they walked away from the table. Will was standing in their way and he dodged and weaved to avoid them. I couldn't help it. I laughed out loud. Bethia and John looked at me and then at each other. John nodded and said, "Yes, I'm ready." With a final wave, they turned and walked slowly through the far wall.

"Holy cow!" cried Will, backing towards me. I stepped away from Dad and grabbed Will's hand, leading him to one side.

The Fossils gathered around Dad all talking at once — already making plans. I don't think Dad was really listening. He was staring at the little Stone in his hands, his face flushed and grim.

Will put his arms around me and I felt the solid warmth of his body. I was glad Dad was holding the Stone. I was glad it wasn't my responsibility, alone.

"Boy," he said, "I wonder what other tricks your Guardian Circle have up their sleeves, huh?"

"Nothing more for a little while, I hope," I said, fervently.

Will, his hands trembling, gripped my shoulders. "Let's leave it up to them, okay?"

I looked at the group of old people round my father. "Dare we?" I asked, with a shaky laugh. And then I shrugged. "Why not?"

Epilogue

A few months have passed since we found the Gregor Stone. Spring is just around the corner and Gladys is poring over seed catalogues. She wants to plant a garden of vegetables and flowers. She finally got a little kitten. She named him Gregory. He doesn't have a single magic trick in his repertoire, but he's awfully cute. So far he hasn't shown any interest in her bird feeder, but one never knows.

Aunt Irene, Mr. Basely, Mitzi and Luther are teaching Dad and me all about the Stone. We've learned some pretty amazing stuff. I'd like to tell you what it is but my lips are sealed. For now, at least.

Dad has gotten really carried away renovating the house. He sold his truck. He'd like to find a job, but the Fossils are discouraging it right now. Things are a lot better between Dad and me. We talk a lot. He even suggested I go and visit Joanna for spring break. I did.

Things haven't changed much on that front. She seems to be really into the art scene in Toronto. Her friends are "big city." She seems happy on her own. She took me sightseeing for the first few days, and then she lost interest and pretty much left me on my own. Like I said before, there are some people who care and some who just don't seem to have it in them. I was glad to get home. I don't think I'm missing much. I've got three mothers at 135. And if I let Mrs. Lennox have her way, I'd end up with four.

I'm a lot happier now. I hardly ever get really angry any more. It's a new feeling, but I'm getting used to it. Believe me, it's not all that easy living with the Fossils. They still worry about me. Dad and I have had to clear the air a few times when they got a bit carried away, checking up on me and generally fussing around. But at least they don't follow me around quite as much. I've had a few Warnings, but they haven't been bad ones. I've found out that they can actually tell me good news, too. Instead of scaring me like they used to, I find myself kind of excited to see what they have to say. Will keeps hoping I'll be able to tell him what his next English Lit mark will be. Poor guy, he may be a math whiz, but Shakespeare does him in every time.

As for Will and me, well, we don't spend too much time talking about what happened. We go to basketball games and movies, and sometimes we play cards with the Fossils. We still argue a lot but I figure that's the way we'll always be.

On the whole, things are pretty good.

Even so, and I try not to pay much attention to it, there's this feeling that hangs over me. Over all of us. That maybe someday, we'll have to face Dunstan Gregor one more time.

About the author

In addition to being a writer, Margaret Buffie is both a teacher and an artist. She has had a lifelong interest in the unexplained and is currently writing a new novel for young people. Margaret Buffie lives with her family in Winnipeg, Manitoba.

Other books by Margaret Buffie

Who Is Frances Rain?

While on summer vacation, 15-year-old Lizzie discovers the remains of an old cabin — and a pair of glasses that forces her to see into the ghostly past.

1988, Honourable Mention, The Canadian Library Association Young Adult Book Award

My Mother's Ghost

Something is happening at Willow Creek Ranch, where 16-year-old Jess and her family moved after the accidental death of her brother. Is Jess seeing things — or are they seeing her?

1992, Shortlisted, The Governor General's Award

Sometimes being a teenager isn't so great ...

Golden Girl and Other Stories
by Gillian Chan

Here in Elmwood, you will find a perfectly ordinary high school. You may even recognize some of the kids.

There's Dennis — safe only as long as the school bully has someone else to torment; and Elly, for whom school is an escape from a suffocating home life.

There's Anna, the golden girl who's not quite as sophisticated as she thinks; and Donna, her best friend, consumed by jealousy and spite.

There's Bob — he uses cruelty to hide his unhappiness; and Andy, who finds an unexpected way to shine.

Come meet them. You'll probably discover you have a lot in common.